Ravaged

Anthony Izzo

Published by White Knuckle Books, 2022.

MW01658531

Copyright © 2022 Anthony Izzo

Published by White Knuckle Books

All rights reserved. No portion of this work may be reproduced in any form without permission from the publisher, except where permitted by United States copyright law. This is a work of fiction. Any resemblance of characters to persons living or dead, is coincidental.

For Jenn, my own constant reader.

One

The car had gone off the road in a blur. Gina's head hurt. The airbag hung on the dash like a deflated balloon. A burning stink filled the vehicle. She touched her head, worried she was bleeding. No blood. That was something. The driver's side door was opened, and Steve had stumbled out into the snow.

Gina got out of the car. The Kia's front end was crumpled. They were in a roadside ditch, pitched forward, and she sloshed through some freezing water as she climbed out. Behind their car, David and Priya's SUV was cockeyed in the ditch.

"Steve, you there?"

"I'm here," he called from the other side of the Kia.

She headed around, where he leaned against a tree. Blood trickled from his lower lip.

"Are you hurt?" she said.

"Just a little banged up. We need to check on David and Priya."

They headed over to the SUV, where David and Priya were climbing out the rear hatch. The deer had come out of nowhere, and the road had been icy. Steve swerved, the Kia fishtailed, and the next thing Gina knew, they'd slammed into the ditch. Unable to stop, the Jeep had joined them.

David wobbled forward. Priya held his arm, steadying him.

"You guys okay?" Gina said.

"Scared shitless, but okay," David said.

"Same," Priya said.

"Looks like we're not making the lodge tonight," Steve said.

They'd been planning this trip for two months. Priya was finally able to get time off from her job as chief of neurosurgery at one of Buffalo's largest hospitals. Same with David. He ran a busy GI practice in the Southtowns.

Steve and Gina had left Tempo in Antonia's hands. She was a more than capable manager. The restaurant would be in good shape with Antonia at the helm. Business was damned good, and they were developing a reputation and one of Buffalo's hottest Italian restaurants. After five years without a vacation, they'd decided to treat themselves.

It was supposed to be the perfect getaway. Except things were off to a lousy start.

"So how far in the middle of nowhere are we?" David said.

"Pretty far," Steve said.

"Did you hit your head?" Priya said.

"The dizziness is his natural state shining through," Steve said.

"I'm serious, David, did you bang your head?" Priya said.

"Neuro docs. Always worried about head injuries" David said. "I'm fine. Neck is a little stiff, but the noggin is good."

Gina took out her phone and checked the maps app. "We're about fifteen minutes from the lodge."

This was their first time staying at the lodge. One of Steve's buddies from high school rented the place out as an Air B and B. He gave them a deal on the place for the week. They were an hour-and-a-half from the city, but the lodge was near a little town called Barker.

"Gonna need Triple A," Steve said.

"Calling," Gina said.

She dug her Triple A card out of the vehicle and called the 800 number. Gina was able to give them a mile marker and the road, which approximated their position. The Triple A rep said it would be between ninety minutes and two hours. That left a lot of time to stand out in the cold.

"Gonna be here a while," Gina said. "They're backed up."

The snow fell heavier, pelting Gina's face.

"Sorry about this, all," Steve said.

"Not your fault, man," David said. "That deer came out of nowhere."

"Is everyone okay?" Priya said.

"Lip's bleeding, but considering, we're lucky," Steve said.

Gina eyed the vehicles. The Kia was trashed and climbing in the SUV might cause it to tip further. They'd need to be towed out with a winch. The Jeep looked drivable. The Kia was going on a flatbed. Once they got to the lodge, Gina would have to call the insurance. While she had called for help, David had called for a tow truck, as well.

"I'm gonna grab our hats and gloves," David said.

"Same," Steve said. "Gotta try and keep warm."

In the time since they'd gone off the road, no traffic had passed. Not that a ride would do much good. They had to wait here for the tow truck.

While they waited for the men to grab hats and gloves, an animal scream burst through the surrounding woods. It sounded like something in extreme pain. "Jesus, that was awful."

"Sounds like it's dying," Priya said.

"The deer ran from that direction. Wonder if it was wounded?"

Steve came back with Gina's winter had and gloves. She put them on. David had done the same for Priya. She slipped on a knit hat, her long, dark hair spilling out from underneath.

"Did you two hear that scream?" David said.

"How could you not?" Gina said.

The sun began to dip. It was almost four-thirty. She didn't love the idea of standing stranded by the road. Gina pulled out her phone searched for anything near their location. A place called Augie's Truck Stop came up. Two miles ahead. "I found a truck stop up the road. It's a few miles."

"Thinking we could shelter there? Someone will have to wait with the vehicles," Steve said.

"You read my mind. Beats sitting in messed-up vehicles," Gina said.

"I'll wait with the vehicles," David said. "I can call you when the tow truck gets here."

"You sure?" Steve said.

"I'm sure. You best bring me a coffee, though."

"I think we can manage that," Priya said. "You're the best."

"Don't let it get around."

Priya kissed him, then turned to David and Gina, saying, "Ready? The walk will warm us up."

"Let's go."

David watched the three of them disappear around the bend in the road. It was full dark now, and he fetched a mini flashlight from the Jeep's console. He shined it on the vehicle. There didn't seem to be any major damage. The one side of the truck had ended up in the ditch, and the Jeep sat cocked at an angle. At least they could still drive it. The Kia had taken it a little worse.

He hoped to see a passing vehicle, even just to know he wasn't out here completely alone. The road was flanked by dense woods. He was a city boy by heart. David had spent his life in Buffalo. Met Priya in med school at the University of Buffalo.

She was the top of her class. She'd been the youngest chief of surgery in the history of her hospital. Not that they were kids. Both would turn forty-five next year. The vacation would be nice. Quiet. Well, except for the shooting part.

Steve and Gina had brought a few guns for target shooting. The plan was to plink some beer cans out back of the lodge. Steve had said something about blasting pumpkins with the shotgun. Did he bring his own or was he going to purchase pumpkins for that purpose? David had neglected to ask.

He crossed his arms for warmth. A gust of wind rocked him, and snow swirled around. That damned tow truck driver had better hurry up.

He paced along the shoulder, thinking movement would warm him up. That's when something thudded against the rear of the jeep. He shined the light and went to check it out.

On the ground lay the head and neck of a deer. The head had been torn from the body. The flesh around the neck was tattered. David recoiled. The deer head had left a smear on the SUV's hatch. A chill rocketed through him.

David shined the light on the woods, but the beam didn't penetrate far. He felt like someone was watching him but he couldn't see them. Now would be a perfect time for a car to pass by. Even better if he could flag them down.

Footsteps crunched in the snow. Someone moving parallel to the road. Who would pull such a sink prank? And why would someone be messing with him? Whoever threw a deer's head would have to be damned strong.

Steve had the guns in his vehicle. He looked down at the deer's head. One glassy eye stared up at him. Was it the same deer that had darted across the road?

"Just so you know, I have a gun!" David said.

No response came.

The footsteps sounded like they were trailing off. Back the way they'd been driving when the accident happened. He caught a whiff of something in the air. Like wet dog mixed with rotten eggs. Definitely some kind of animal. But what the hell kind of animal would throw a deer's head at a truck?

He backed closer to the Kia and popped the hatch. Because the Kia had tipped downward, the cargo inside had slid forward and pressed against the back seat. He saw the long gun bag and managed to wrestle it out.

After unzipping the bag, he slipped the shotgun out. Steve had some shells tucked in a holder affixed to the stock. David clicked a few shells home and racked the pump. Flipped the safety to red.

If it's red, you're dead. That he remembered from the few times he'd gone shooting.

A deep roar echoed from the woods. Something damned big made that noise. He aimed the shotgun in the direction of the woods, sweeping it back and forth. His own ragged breathing filled his ears. "Stay in the woods, whatever you are."

He stood there with the shotgun for what seemed like forever. The woods had gone silent. The wind howled. His heart pounded.

David lowered the gun and took out his cell and dialed Steve's number. Steve answered on the third ring.

"Miss us already?"

"If you could hurry your asses back here, that would be appreciated."

"Tow truck there already?"

"No, but something else is."

"What's that mean?"

David filled him in on the deer's head and the strange roar.

"A whole deer's head?"

"That's what I said. I got your shotgun out of the Kia."

"We're almost to the truck stop. We'll grab some hot drinks and head right back. You okay man?"

"Rattled, but okay. Whatever made that noise sounded huge."

"All right. Sit tight and we'll be there soon."

David ended the call. They couldn't get here soon enough.

Two

The truck stop was a bust. Gina felt deflated. The place was abandoned. The pumps had been removed and only the overhead canopy remained. A mini mart and attached restaurant building stood dark. Unfortunately, the web search hadn't said anything about the place being closed.

A sign in the mini-mart's window advertised homemade pies. The pie would've tasted good with a hot cup of coffee.

"Looks like we're too late," Steve said.

"By a few years," Gina said.

The sign out front read UGIE'S. The A was missing.

Screw you, UGIE'S, I wanted pie.

Gina noticed some graffiti sprayed on the side of the building. It was in the shape of a crude monster with triangular claws, the arms raised above its head. "That's an odd piece of art."

Below the crude artwork were the words: *Shut you down*.

Priya said, "Wonder when this place closed?"

"A while ago from the look of it," Gina said.

"We should get back to David. He sounded pretty freaked out," Steve said.

Something rustled behind the mini-mart. A man in a long, olive green coat appeared around the corner. He wore a loose stocking cap on his head. He approached the three of them, hands in pockets.

"Can we help you?" Gina said.

The man stopped a few feet short of them. The odor of gasoline wafted off him. "Didn't you know this place was closed?"

Gina said, "We're not from the area. Our car broke down."

"What's your story?" Steve said.

"I live around here. Right back there," he said, turning and pointing at the truck stop. "Name's Roland."

Priya said, "You live behind there? Are you okay?"

"Oh, I'm fine. Got a nice little tent. Going to be moving on soon, though. Things getting weird around here," he said, scratching his beard stubble.

"What's with that graffiti?" Gina said.

"That there's the reason this place closed. Weird happenings. Truckers got spooked. Something walking around their trucks at night, banging on doors."

Gina glanced at the crude graffiti again. It did resemble some sort of furry monster. "Are we talking about a Sasquatch?"

The man touched a finger to the tip of his nose. "You win the prize, ma'am. Not hanging around here much longer. I can smell it in the air."

She found it hard to believe an entire truck stop closed because people got spooked by a mythical monster. "Is that really what happened?"

"Augie Peters claims he saw it. Closing up one night. Nearly bashed in the door and came for him. That was it for Augie. Put it up for sale the next week."

Roland seemed lucid. She didn't detect alcohol on him and he didn't seem high. "Where will you go?"

"I'll move down the road. There's a shelter run by the Baptists in Barker. Stay there for the winter. It'll be safe. Where you folks going?"

"Headed up to a friend's lodge near Barker. About fifteen miles south of here."

Roland shook his head slowly. "I don't recommend that. Not at all. That's its territory."

"Roland, we appreciate it, but I think we'll be fine," Priya said. "Can we offer you some money?"

Roland put a hand up, as if to ward it off. "I don't take handouts. Got everything I need, and if I don't have it, I can get it. I appreciate you folks, though. Well, I'm gonna go hunker down in the tent. Getting cold and I'm hitting the road first thing. Don't linger," he said, heading back toward the store.

"You really think someone got spooked and closed this place down?" Steve said.

"It was likely the economy. Doesn't seem like it's booming around here," Priya said.

"Hope he's going to be all right," Gina said.

"Seems like a survivor," Steve said. "We should get back to David. Make sure he's okay."

David got tired of looking at the deer's head and decided to drag it to the side of the road. It would look odd when the tow truck driver got here if a deer's head was lying around. Flashlight clamped between his teeth, he hunkered and grabbed the head, one hand on top and the other under the jaw.

The damn thing smelled horrible. He dragged it out of the ditch and left it at the wood's edge. For good measure, he shined the light in the woods. It was then he noticed the footprint, right next to a thick pine tree.

He inched closer, not wanting to get too close, as if the woods could reach out and grab him. The print was close to eighteen inches long. Vaguely human-shaped. Five distinct toes.

"This is getting fucking weird," David said.

Someone had to be playing a prank out here. Maybe messing with passing motorists. Possibly saw them having trouble and decided to have some fun.

But who has fun by tossing a severed animal head at people?

Someone with a fake foot must've made that print. Although that same someone would've been awfully strong to toss a deer head.

He was relieved when he heard voices. Priya, Gina, and Steve appeared around the bend. To his dismay, they weren't carrying coffee or snacks.

Gina spotted David's flashlight beam. He was standing near the Jeep at the side of the ditch.

"No coffee? Did you bastards drink it all?" David said.

"Truck stop is abandoned. Shut down," Gina said.

"Well don't that suck," David said.

"You would've just had to piss, anyway," Steve said.

They joined David near the Jeep. Priya took his hand.

"What's this about a deer's head?" she said.

"I dragged it out of the ditch. It's over there," David said, pointing at the woods. "There's a big ass footprint over there, too. "

"Let me see the light," Steve said. "I want to see this."

David handed over the flashlight. Gina and Priya joined Steve in crossing the ditch. The deer's head, followed by a blood trail, lay in the snow. Steve shined the light along the ground.

"I'll be damned. Look at that," Steve said.

Whoever owned the print was huge. The image of the crude monster graffiti and Roland's story echoed in Gina's mind. "Has to be someone playing a prank."

Priya said, "That deer head is a long way to go for a prank."

"Then what threw the head?"

A long whooping cry echoed through the woods. Gina felt her arm hairs stand at attention. It didn't sound close, but it was no less unnerving. "Let's get back to the vehicles. And the shotgun."

Back at the vehicles, David handed Steve the shotgun. Gina couldn't wait for the tow truck driver to get here.

Roland huddled in his tent and zipped up the sleeping bag. He'd pitched the tent between a dumpster and a stack of pallets at the truck stop's rear. It gave him a good buffer from the wind. He hoped those people got back on the road. It wasn't safe to be wandering around.

Roland was taking a chance spending another night out here. He'd intended to start the trek toward the homeless shelter in Barker, but he'd been tired. Food had been scarce. He'd eaten the last can of cold stew and some beef jerky this morning. The malnutrition was sapping his energy, and he'd napped most of the day.

The mini-mart and truck stop's lot backed up to the woods. He supposed he could find a way into the old truck stop hotel if things got hairy out here. Last night, he'd heard something smashing wood among the trees. It hadn't gotten close, but when he opened the tent flap to look out, he got the sense something watched back.

He thought about his brother Alex's offer. *Just call me, Roland. I have a job waiting for you. I'll put you up at our place until you get on your feet.*

Roland hadn't talked to Alex in almost six months. The shelter had a phone and allowed you the occasional call. He still had Alex's number written on a Tim Horton's napkin. Maybe he'd make that call.

How long had it been since he'd slept in a warm bed that wasn't owned by a shelter? Or eaten a hot meal without five other people at a cheap, plastic table. He'd been living this life for six years. Lydia had kicked him out. Soon after, he'd gotten laid off from his job as a welder and couldn't afford his apartment.

From there, it was living in his Subaru. Couldn't find a job – and wasn't really trying, to be honest. The car was repossessed. He'd taken to the street, bouncing in and out of shelters. Managed to beg for bus fare and headed out to God's country, where he alternated between camping and shelters.

He'd bought the tent and sleeping bag at an AmVets thrift store using money he'd panhandled. It wasn't too bad sleeping in there until it got consistently below freezing. But maybe it was time to get back to living in the world.

A shiver passed through Roland. He wiggled deeper into the sleeping bag. The wind snapped the tent.

He was a little nervous sleeping behind Augie's. Those people who'd stopped probably thought him an unbalanced homeless guy. But Augie – who sometimes gave Roland day old sandwiches and free coffee – had been scared to death. Same went for the truckers. They bypassed Augie's after that thing started showing up here at night.

One trucker from Tennessee awoke to his door being thumped. When he got out to check, a fist-sized dent had been punched in the door. A driver bunking in the attached hotel claimed someone large with deep, red eyes stared in his window.

And then Augie himself had seen something. Too bad. He was a good man. Plus, he fed Roland on a regular basis, no judgement or questions asked.

Roland wasn't tired, so he decided to read. He took out a flashlight and a battered copy of *Dune* he'd lifted from a library. Wasn't particularly proud of that, but he'd loved *Dune* as a kid. One of the few books that really grabbed him. He'd wanted to read it again.

He'd read about three pages when he heard the footsteps approaching the tent. He shut off the light, as not to reveal himself. Then he cocked an ear to listen.

Someone had stopped near the tent. He heard deep breathing, and then an animal-like chuffing noise. He began to shiver in the sleeping bag, but not from the cold. Roland's teeth chattered. Could whoever was outside the tent hear that?

Man murdered when killer heard chattering teeth.

Whatever was outside the tent came closer. He got the sense it was only a few feet away. Roland closed his eyes, as if it would make the intruder cease to exist. "Go away," he whispered.

A deep sniffing noise came from outside the tent.

Is it trying to catch my scent? Or has it already?

He heard it pace back and forth, low growls and grunts coming from the beast. It let out a roar that felt like a chest punch, then banged the metal dumpster. After that, he heard it run off.

Roland guessed it was frustrated at not being able to find him. He wanted to pack up his tent and just run, but he found he was too scared to move. Instead, he lay on his side and pulled the sleeping bag halfway over his head, leaving room to breathe.

Please don't come back.

Three

The flatbed driver had gotten Priya and David's Jeep out of the ditch with a winch. The driver was loading the Kia on to the flatbed. Gina, with the help of the others, had transferred all their gear to the Jeep, which was still drivable. The Kia was going to a repair garage in Barker.

The driver hopped in the flatbed's cab, beeped twice, and pulled onto the road. What a damned mess.

"You ready to get back on the road?"

Gina checked her watch. It was a little past seven PM. "Been ready for a while."

The four of them hopped in the Jeep. Priya drove. The snow pelted the windshield. Gina hadn't checked the weather reports near Barker, but there'd been steady snow.

"So what do you think did that to the deer?" David said.

"Had to have been a large predator," Steve said.

"But why throw it?" Gina said.

"Maybe it was shaking the head in its jaws or something," Steve said. "And it flew out."

"It'd have to be something huge. A big bear."

Priya said, "And that doesn't explain the footprint."

"Maybe it was a genuine Bigfoot," Gina said.

Steve said, "Maybe he brought the Loch Ness monster with him."

"Shut up. I'm serious," Gina said.

"Even if it was, we left it behind," Priya said. "You'll have a really cool story to tell."

"David Reilly, Bigfoot hunter," Steve said.

"All I know is it sounded huge. Glad to be on the road and headed for a hot meal and some beers," David said.

They drove for a half hour before finding the cabin's driveway. It was marked by a mailbox at the end and a wooden sign with the name

CARVER etched into it. They took the long driveway back to the cabin. Gina discovered that calling it cabin was an understatement.

It was a large, log home with an attached three-car garage. The front of the place had floor-to-ceiling windows. The online description had indicated four bedrooms and three baths. The place had to be four or five thousand square feet. Pictures hadn't done it justice.

"Damn, you got fancy friends," David said.

"We've got our own ski lodge," Steve said.

There was a firepit with Adirondack chairs arranged in a circle in the front yard. Mostly snow-covered. Priya pulled up to the garage and killed the engine.

"Let's get unloaded and eat," Priya said.

Steve unlocked the front door while Gina and the others grabbed luggage and the food from the back of the Jeep. Gina hauled her bag and a few grocery bags inside. The main floor was an open design. The kitchen flowed into a great room, complete with a pool table and small bar area. A stone fireplace dominated one wall. This was going to be nice.

Steve checked out the fireplace. "Gas insert. No wood chopping required. I like it."

He fiddled with the fireplace control mounted on the wall and the flame whooshed to life. Steve and David took the luggage upstairs while Gina and Priya unpacked the coolers with the food in it. The kitchen had some top-of-the-line stainless steel appliances, including an eight-burner range.

They had some nice strip steaks to cook up. Gina had to call the insurance about the Kia. First, she'd eat. Her stomach felt like it was folding in on itself.

As she was putting food away in the fridge, she heard the howl. Gina had been hunched over, but she stood up straight. Priya froze, a box of Club crackers in hand. Her eyes were wide.

"What was that?" Priya said.

"Creepy whatever it was."

"It didn't sound close."

The French doors off the kitchen led to a large deck. Gina went and checked the locks. They were secured.

David came bounding downstairs and crossed into the kitchen. "That howl. That's what I heard."

Steve joined them a moment later. The four of them stood motionless in the kitchen. The howl came again, seeming to echo through the woods. It sounded sad and lonely to Gina. That didn't make it any less creepy.

"I'm glad I brought guns," Steve said.

"I don't think it'll come to that," Priya said. "There's lots of wildlife out here, I'm sure."

"At least it sounds far away," David said.

"It comes any closer, we're ready for it," Steve said.

"Take it easy, cowboy," Priya said, setting the box of crackers on the counter.

"Just saying, it doesn't hurt to be prepared."

Steve had never shot anything other than some hay bales and beer cans they'd used for target practice. Gina couldn't see him blasting away at the wildlife. Still, she felt better knowing they had the guns. Just in case. "How about we get those steaks cooking and get down to drinking? Everyone will feel better."

"Should we invite Sasquatch for dinner?" Steve said.

"Screw you, man. I'm taking the biggest steak, just for that comment," David said.

Four

"Snow's picking up pretty good," Monique said, pulling the truck into the hotel lot. "Hope we can get out and do our investigation."

"It's just a little snow," James said from the passenger seat.

"I don't fancy going out there if we can't see," Kurt said from the back seat. Monique glanced in the rearview. Kurt had his legs crossed and was looking at his phone.

"What's good, Kurt?" Monique said.

"National Weather Service storm warning. High winds. Blowing snow. Travel difficult to impossible staring tomorrow evening," Kurt said.

Kurt usually acted like he was wearing barbed wire underwear. Like a cranky old man, although he was only forty-five, twenty years Monique and James' senior.

"That still gives us time," James said. "Suck it up, old man."

"Youth is wasted on the young," Kurt said.

Despite Kurt's demeanor, he was a valuable part of the team. He knew outdoors stuff better than anyone. An experienced hunter and camper, he was also a survivalist. He just happened to have an interest in Bigfoot research after having two encounters of his own.

Monique had only experienced vocalizations on an expedition in a remote area of Pennsylvania. James was yet to experience any of it, but they'd formed a good team. Sightings had increased in the Barker area. Sightings that went back sixty years.

"Let's go check in," James said. "I'm freezing."

The heat in the truck had been dribbling out. Monique would have to get that fixed soon. The three of them grabbed overnight bags and headed to the hotel lobby. Behind the counter was a cardboard cutout of a cartoon Sasquatch, a snarl on its face.

The desk clerk, a hipster-looking guy with a waxed mustache, looked up and said, "Can I help you?"

"Two rooms under Patterson," Monique said.

The clerk typed in her last name. "Monique?"

"That's me."

"I'll need a credit card and a photo ID."

Monique dug in her purse, then handed him her license and a Mastercard. The clerk took them. His mustache glistened with some sort of wax, and pomade had been applied liberally to his dark, wavy hair. He ran her credit card and put her license through a small scanner. "Ever have any experience with your guest there?"

The clerk turned and glanced at the cardboard Sasquatch. Rolled his eyes. "That's the owner's idea. Thankfully we're not a Bigfoot-themed hotel. I've never seen anything, but people complain about animal noises."

He handed back Monique's credit card and license.

"We're here to do some research on Sasquatch."

"Like one of those reality shows?" the clerk said.

Those shows had given legit researchers a bad name. Monique and the others were part of the Northeast Bigfoot Organization. They had zoologists and biologists who were a part of the organization. They weren't some crackpot team who ran around with night vision cameras thinking they'd glimpsed a Sasquatch. "Those guys are frauds."

"And you're not?" the clerk said.

"Hey, take it easy," James said.

"I got this," Monique said. "We take our research seriously. We operate with data, not superstition or speculation. And we aren't some half-assed reality show."

"If you say so," the clerk said, sliding their room cards over the counter. "Rooms one-ten and one-thirteen. First hallway on the left. Happy Bigfoot hunting," he said in a sing-song voice.

Arrogant bastard, aren't you? She should be used to it by now. "Yeah, happy Bigfoot hunting."

Monique and James got settled in their room. James' parents wouldn't approve of them sharing a room. His father was a Baptist pastor, the fire-and-brimstone type. James had to assure his father they were getting separate rooms. Monique's parents were cool in that regard. They recognized her as a twenty-five-year-old adult with her own life.

"My parents would be shitting right now if they knew," James said.

"Well they're not here, are they?"

"My Dad's wound pretty tight."

"Is he still hoping you follow in his footsteps?"

"Yeah, that conversation comes up once a month."

"Keep doing your art, baby. Don't let him talk you out of it."

James was an incredible artist. He worked a day job stocking at Target. The dream was to do comics full time, and he'd done his own indie comic book and raised nearly twenty thousand with a Kickstarter. James' father, Ray, would say things like, "Why don't you get a solid job like your girlfriend?"

Monique was the youngest VP/Regional Manager for the largest supermarket chain on the East Coast. She'd risen from cashier, starting at sixteen. She never liked when Ray would bring that up. He'd say things like: "Why can't you be more like your girlfriend? She's going places." She'd see the shame on James' face, even though he had nothing to be ashamed about.

She liked Ray Garland about as much as she liked bee stings. James' mom had died when he was ten. Ray hadn't remarried.

James sat on the edge of the bed. Monique sat next to him, their thighs touching. She could feel the tension thrumming through him. "Hey, relax. This is going to be great."

"Yeah, I know," he said, leaning forward, elbows propped on his thighs. She traced small circles on the back of his neck.

"I can help you relax," she said, leaning in and kissing his neck, inhaling the scent of his soap. A nice, clean smell. He didn't wear cologne, and she appreciated that. Some guys marinated in the stuff.

"Sounds good," he said, sitting up and turning to kiss her. His hand went to her leg, and he stroked her inner thigh. She moaned and kissed him hard. They lay back on the bed and she rolled on top of him, straddling him. Monique took off her top and unhooked her bra. James' caressed her breasts.

She threw her head back and moaned. This was hell of a nice start to the trip.

After, they lay in bed, Monique on her back, James on his side with his arm draped across her belly. They'd been loud. She'd been loud. Didn't care, though. No one knew them here.

"That was amazing," she said.

"Better than amazing."

"That guy at the desk was an ass," she said.

"No one understands what we do. I stopped expecting people to get it."

"This area's hot with sightings. I feel good about this one."

"Feel better with Kurt's big ass guns along."

"We're not here to hunt it."

"Just saying. They can be aggressive. The one around here is, if the reports are right," James said.

The Barker Monster, as it had been dubbed, didn't seem to avoid humans. Just the opposite. There had been reports of it killing small dogs, peering in windows, and in one instance, attempting to open a resident's back door. Kurt had guns, if needed, although Monique didn't like the idea of going out to kill a Sasquatch. She wanted to study them, not kill them. Although if they ever came across an angry Sasquatch, being prepared was advised.

"So we should get up early, maybe follow up on sightings, then talk to people in town before the weather goes to shit," she said.

"If we're going out in the woods, we do it early."

Someone knocked on their door. Kurt would've texted if he needed something. Monique got dressed and looked through the peephole. A burly cop in a winter jacket stood at the door.

She turned to James and said, "Might want to get dressed. Police."

"All ready? Damn."

James hopped out of bed and hurried into his clothes. The police knocked again. They usually ended up getting a visit from local police before an investigation. Got a warning about not trespassing or harassing residents.

Monique opened the door.

"Good evening, Miss. Lieutenant Rodgers, Barker PD."

"Did we do something wrong, officer?"

"You're the Bigfoot people."

"We are," Monique said.

"What are your plans while you're in town?"

"I think that's our business," Monique said.

"I'm asking because the group we had up here a few years ago caused some problems," Rodgers said. "Ended up trespassing. Homeowner armed himself. It ended peacefully, but you can see why I'm concerned."

"We know to stay off private property."

"I'm sure you do. Just don't trespass and try not to harass people in town. If they want to talk to you, fine, but I don't like pushy."

The Lieutenant had found them quickly. "How did you know we were in town?"

"Barker's small. Everyone knows everyone. Word gets around, especially when Bigfoot people show up."

The hotel clerk must've alerted someone. Intentional or not, they'd have to be careful not to piss off the police. "We'll obey all the local laws, sheriff."

"Lieutenant. Sheriff's are county."

"Right, Lieutenant. We're not in trouble?"

"No. Just a courtesy visit. Are you carrying firearms?"

She wasn't obligated to tell him that Kurt had guns, but it might save them trouble. "The other member of our group has guns, just in case."

"Just be safe with them."

"The guns aren't a problem?"

"I would recommend them if you're going out there."

"How so?" Monique said.

She realized James was now standing behind her. "Have you seen anything, officer?"

"Let's say I'm a believer. And be careful out there. Enjoy your stay in Barker," he said, and started down the hallway.

Monique stuck her head out the door and said, "Any chance of an interview?"

"Not gonna happen," he said, not stopping.

Footsteps woke Roland. He was still cocooned in his sleeping bag. Although awake, he kept his eyes shut, as if it would ward off the footsteps. He remained still in the sleeping bag. A low growl rumbled outside the tent.

Go away. Go away.

It wasn't going away, though. The footsteps drew closer, and that familiar stink was back. Another growl came, and it was just outside the tent. He was easy prey lying here. The only other time he'd been this scared was when a junkie had held a knife to his throat under a railroad bridge. He'd taken Roland's shoes and twenty-three dollars.

Roland shook inside the sleeping bag. He willed himself to stop, but it was like having a runaway case of the chills.

He heard heavy breathing outside the tent. On the other side of the flap. Roland had a backpack with him. In it was a hunting knife that he kept just in case. He'd picked it up after the junkie had held the knife on him. Wasn't getting robbed again after the bridge incident.

The footsteps headed away from the tent. He reached one arm out of the sleeping bag and wriggled the knife out of the pack. He got out of the sleeping bag in case he had to run. Roland hunkered in the tent. It was still thudding around. Sounded like it was pacing the lot, maybe agitated it couldn't find him.

He had a decision to make. If it came close to the tent again, it might figure out Roland was inside. Or what if it left and came back again?

Roland inched to the tent flap. He slowly unzipped the flap and peered out. He saw it standing in the moonlight. The massive, sloped shoulders. The too-long, muscular arms. Damned thing was well over seven feet tall.

No way could he outrun the creature. Wouldn't make it fifty feet. But if it came for him in the tent, he stood no chance. The creature turned and glared at him with large, red eyes. It roared. Felt like the whole tent shook.

Roland grabbed his pack, unzipped the flap all the way, and scurried out of the tent. The beast charged. He spotted a ladder bolted to the side of the building for roof access. He could never beat the creature in a footrace. Its stride was too long.

Instead, he hurried up the ladder and hopped onto the mini-mart's roof. The monster reached the ladder. It placed a foot on the ladder and gripped the side rails. As it stepped and pulled, the ladder gave with a screech. The bolts holding it in popped, and the bottom rung bent.

Damned thing had to weigh four or five-hundred pounds. Thank the Lord for small favors. Furious, the Bigfoot ripped the ladder the rest of the way out. It tossed the bent ladder across the lot, where it clanged against the asphalt.

He was high enough where it couldn't grab the roof's edge and climb up. At least he hoped. The thing was basically an overpowered ape, wasn't it?

The creature thumped the wall and screamed. Roland backed away from the edge and hunkered in the center of the roof. He heard it banging around, possibly smashing fists against the dumpster. After a few moments, he watched it stalk off into the woods, and its roars diminished.

He wasn't getting off the roof until daylight. After clearing away an inch of snow, he took a spare blanket from his pack and wrapped it around himself. He'd survive. There'd been plenty of nights colder than this where he'd holed up under an overpass or in an abandoned building.

Roland kept his gaze on the woods. There'd be no sleeping tonight. Maybe it'd decided he wasn't worth the effort.

Five

Gina had a full belly and was beginning to doze on the sectional near the cabin's fireplace. Priya and David were shooting pool. After dinner, she'd called the insurance and reported the accident. Steve was scrolling through his phone, a look of grim concentration on his face.

She sat up, not wanting to doze off. Studied Steve. "What's so interesting?"

"This area is apparently a Bigfoot hotspot."

Gina and Steve had jumped at the chance to rent the lodge. They hadn't planned on leaving the property much and hadn't researched nearby Barker, or the surrounding area. "Seriously?"

"Yeah, going back to the sixties. They routinely get Bigfoot researchers up here."

David, leaning over to line up a shot, said, "Maybe that explains my encounter."

"When was the most recent sighting?" Priya said.

"Two-thousand-eighteen," Steve said. "Report of a large intruder out by someone's chicken coop."

"Could've been an overgrown fox," Gina said.

"Article says a lady called nine-one-one and reported a large, hairy human-figure near her chicken coop. When the cops got there, it was gone, but it had slaughtered ten chickens."

She didn't think Bigfoot would be a concern on vacation. The biggest worry she wanted on the trip was whether to have her steak medium rare or rare.

"Here's another one about a cop who saw something on two legs cross the road in front of his cruiser."

Priya said, "Maybe they should send one of those bigfoot-hunting teams from reality television. Mountain guys or something like that."

Gina laughed, but she was still unnerved. They'd all seen the deer's head and heard the strange howls. "We should've reported the deer."

"A dead deer?" Steve said.

"A *decapitated* deer," Gina said. "Little different."

"Still, it's an animal. Deer get hit on the road all the time," Steve said.

"They might've viewed it differently given the area's history," Gina said.

Steve set his phone down. "I shouldn't have brought it up. Let's just have fun."

She wanted to enjoy the vacation, but things had gotten off to a rough start. First, they had the accident, then David had a strange encounter. To top it off, those eerie howls had echoed outside. She hoped not to hear them again.

The upstairs bathroom had a nice, sunken tub near a bay window that overlooked the woods. A hot bath and a beer sounded good. Great way to unwind. "Gonna go try out that bathtub."

"Want company?" Steve said.

"I'll fly solo this time, but I like your energy," she said, getting up and heading for the stairs.

Gina got undressed in the bedroom and slipped on her robe. She had a bottle of *Lets Go Pils* from one of Buffalo's local breweries and a copy of Stephen Graham Jones' *Night of the Mannequins.* Their bedroom and the other main both had en suites. She headed into the adjoining bathroom. The shower seemed big enough to accommodate four people. At some point, she'd suggest Steve join her in the shower. Lots of room to have fun in there.

She cranked the faucets. Outside, snow whipped in front of the window. The pines went on for miles, gently sloping up a hill. When the bath was ready, she slipped out of the robe and set the beer on the tub, next to her book.

Gina slipped into the water and took a sip of the icy beer. Damn, that tasted good. She closed her eyes and rested her head on the back of the tub. Let every muscle in her body relax.

She took another swig of beer. She closed her eyes again and was drifting off when another howl came from outside. Gina sat up in the tub and looked out the window. Through the snow, near the tree line, she saw a human-like shape. Big. Fur-covered.

Gina gasped and climbed out of the tub and toweled off in hurry. She threw on the robe, knocking her book into the water. "Goddammit," she said, scooping the sodden book from the tub.

She threw the book on the floor. From the hallway came shouting and the sound of someone thumping down the stairs. Gina slipped into the hallway and padded down the stairs. In the great room, Steve was threading shells into the shotgun.

"I saw something out by the tree line," Gina said. "From the bathroom window."

"It sounded close," Steve said. "Ran up and got the shotgun while you were in the bathroom."

David and Priya were going around shutting off lights and checking locks. In a few moments, the lodge was plunged into darkness.

"Good idea turning off the lights," Gina said. "We want to be able to see outside."

"Did you see anything?" Steve said. "When you were checking the windows?"

"Nothing," Priya said. "Just blowing snow."

"We should call the cops," David said.

"And tell them what? It was an animal?" Steve said.

"You're the one standing there with a shotgun, man," David said.

"What did you see exactly?" Priya said.

"A big, dark shape. On two legs. Furry," Gina said.

Steve went to the French doors in the kitchen and Gina followed him. She peered outside, but all she could see was blowing snow and the vague shapes of the trees beyond. She hoped it would keep its distance from the lodge. The glass doors would do nothing to stop an animal of that size if it wanted to get in.

"Don't see anything," Steve said.

"It was standing right near the tree line."

"I'll keep the shotgun handy."

"I'm getting the semiautomatic out," Gina said.

They had a nine-millimeter semiautomatic in addition to the shotgun. At home, they'd kept the guns in a safe, as required by law. This would be the first time they'd kept a gun out for protection.

"If it is what we think, Sasquatches don't usually attack people do they? At least in the accounts of sightings," Priya said.

"This one might," Gina said. "If what Steve read off his phone was accurate."

"Do we want to stay here?" David said.

"Well we're here at least for the night," Steve said. "If there is something roaming around, I think we're fine indoors."

"Unless it comes up to the house. Bears break into houses," Priya said.

"If it does, we have the guns," Gina said.

That wouldn't make her sleep any easier tonight. They agreed to keep the lights off for now and use flashlights. Gina headed back upstairs and drained the tub, lamenting her now soggy book. She picked the book up and squeezed some of the water out.

She shook the book and water sloughed off it. If she let it dry out, it would be readable. Still partially wet, she slipped out of the robe toweled the rest of her body off. Then she got dressed in the adjoining bedroom.

A look out the bedroom window didn't reveal anything new. Just blowing snow. It was picking up out there. The wind gusted, screaming through the lodge's eaves. The weather might not allow them to leave, even if they wanted to go.

Roland awoke on the roof to howling wind and blowing snow. Snow had piled up on him during the night and he brushed it off. He stood up and glanced at the sky. Solid gray. The snow stung his face and got in his eyes. He needed to find shelter.

He went to the roof's edge and looked down. His tent was in ribbons, and his sleeping bag had been tossed aside. At least the bag was still in one piece, and he planned on taking it with. There was no sign of the creature. No fresh prints in the snow.

There'd be no climbing down the ladder. Enough snow had fallen to cushion him. He'd have to jump. In order to land properly, you had to put your feet close together. Created a more stable base. Cover your head with your arms. He'd read that somewhere a long time ago.

He jumped, tucking and rolling in the snow. He came to rest on his back. Managed not to hurt himself. Roland rolled up the sleeping bag and fastened it to his backpack. After scanning the woods, he felt secure that the beast wasn't nearby.

Roland headed out to the road and began the trek towards Barker.

Roland managed to flag down a pick-up truck. The driver let him ride in the bed, and he made it to Barker. The Hope Center was in the main business district, sandwiched between a one-screen movie theater and a Rite Aid. It was an old Boys and Girls Club building. The gymnasium was used for cots, and the other portions of the building were used to serve food. They also functioned as the center's offices.

He headed down the street and entered the center. He saw a familiar face. Dolly Tucker, her white hair cut in a bob, sat at the front desk. She wore one of her customary pastel turtlenecks and a large broach pinned to her chest. "Hey there, stranger. Haven't seen you in a while."

"Been on the road."

"You're soaking wet, Roland. We got some new donations in. I'm sure we have some clothes in your size."

"I appreciate it."

"Kenny's making minestrone as we speak. Get you a hot cup of soup and warm up. Where'd you sleep last night?

"On the roof at Augie's Truck Stop."

He wasn't going to tell her about the encounter with the creature.

Dolly gave him a stern look. "We're open twenty-four hours, you know. I won't ask why you slept on a roof."

"Long story. Won't do that again."

"Get out of those wet clothes before you get pneumonia."

"Will do."

He headed into the center and found the donation room. There were shelves and shelves of folded clothing, free for the taking. No questions asked. Roland searched the shelves until he found a pair of worn-in jeans, a sweater, and a package of socks. He ripped open the pack and took two pair. Wet feet could mean living or dying on the street. He'd known of two guys who lost a foot to frostbite.

Roland changed in the bathroom. They had a laundry facility where he could dry his clothes, as well. For now, he folded them and put them in a plastic shopping bag. Then he headed to the gymnasium, where rows of cots were set up. He took an empty cot next to the wall, adjacent to the boys' locker room door. Set his pack and clothing down.

He didn't worry about theft here like he did in the bigger, city shelters. His stomach gurgled, and he decided to seek out soup and then make that call to Alex.

Roland was ready to get back to some sort of normal life.

Six

Jesse Pinkowski was on his third cup of coffee when Rosco started acting skittish. The Samoyed was standing at the bay window, paws on the sill, and whining. Rosco had been out twice. He should've been all set until around noon.

Jesse sipped his coffee. Rosco could wait a minute. Although the dog could be a pain in the ass, he was grateful for Rosco. Retirement was lonely with Ella gone. Two years since cancer had taken her and the house was now quiet as hell, even with Rosco around.

The past week there'd been some noises outside during the night. His garbage cans had been tossed around by some sort of animal. And something had torn out a section of the fence. Maybe it was a bear. He'd have to get a fence company out here to repair the chain link.

Rosco barked, sharper this time. Wouldn't stop.

"All right, I'm coming, you furry ass pain."

Jesse got up from the table and scratched behind Rosco's ears. He went to the back door and got his boots on. Normally, he'd let Rosco out and the dog would come back inside. Today, he wanted to see what had Rosco riled up.

He opened the back door and Rosco scampered into the yard, which backed up to the woods. Jesse's nearest neighbor was five hundred yards away. Nice and private here, but he sometimes he felt isolated.

Rosco hit the fence and put his front paws up on the rail, right near where the chain link had been ripped away. He barked like there were a herd of cats in the woods. What was driving him so crazy?

Jesse grabbed his quilted flannel and a winter hat from the house. He stepped into the whipping snow, squinting to see Rosco. He crossed the yard until he was standing next to Rosco. Jesse peered at the woods. It was dark in there and between the snow and the darkness, he couldn't see crap.

"What's got you riled up? How about you take care of business and we go inside?"

The hole in the fence didn't concern him as far as Rosco. He was a well-mannered dog and wouldn't go beyond the fence line. Still, he kept yapping. Jesse grabbed his collar and pulled him back from the fence. "Come on if you're not going to go."

He tried dragging Rosco back, but the dog lunged and began snarling. Something really had him fired up. As he backed Rosco from the fence, he saw the source. Between two large pines stood a large, two-legged beast covered in black, matted fur. Jesse felt his blood go cold.

He'd lived here all his life and was aware of the stories, the supposed sightings. Jesse thought them largely bullshit, until now. Unless some big bastard in a monkey suit was pranking him. That wasn't likely.

Rosco growled and bared his teeth. No way was he letting Rosco go after whatever stood in the woods. Jesse managed to drag Rosco back into the house. He slammed the door and locked it. From the back window, he watched the big bastard creep from the woods.

It started toward the house, taking long strides. Jesse felt like his heart might pop out of his chest. He might be joining Ella if that thing broke into the house.

He grabbed his cell phone off the table. Dialed nine-one-one. As it rang, he watched the monstrous thing step over the fence. Now he knew what had destroyed the section of fence in the first place.

Jesse grabbed Rosco's leash off a hook near the door and clipped it to his collar. The phone held to his ear, the nine-one-one dispatcher answered.

"What's your emergency?"

"There's something huge coming toward my house."

"An intruder, sir? Or is it an animal?"

"It's big and walking on two legs. I don't know what it is, just send someone!"

The monster was almost to the house. He didn't have time to mess around on the phone. He ended the call, knowing they would have his address and would send police out regardless.

His initial plan had been to run for his truck out in the driveway. There'd never be enough time. Instead, he headed upstairs, dragging Rosco along with him. Once upstairs, he opened the door to the walk-up attic.

He hurried up to the attic with Rosco in tow. The staircase was narrow. If the monster found its way inside, it would have to find him first, then squeeze up the narrow stairs.

From downstairs came the sound of smashing glass. Then a huge bang, followed by a roar.

Jesse had an old queen mattress leaning against the wall. He scurried under the mattress, which functioned as a lean-to. He hugged Rosco close, the dog whining. "Shhh. Got to be quiet boy."

More smashing and breaking of glass came from downstairs. Jesse closed his eyes. Rosco seemed to understand the need for silence. He buried his head in Jesse's chest, and Jesse stroked the dog's head.

He heard brakes squeal outside, then a car door thumping. That'd better be the police. After a moment, the smashing noises stopped and the house was quiet. He remained frozen in place, Rosco in his arms.

"Barker Police! Is anyone here?"

"Thank God, buddy," Jesse said, scratching behind Rosco's ears.

Jesse slid out from behind the mattress and headed down the attic stairs. He paused for a moment and said, "Hello?"

"Mr. Pinkowski? Is that you?"

"It is. I'm coming downstairs."

Downstairs, Lieutenant Rodgers stood in the kitchen, a shotgun in hand. The back door had been smashed in, the door frame in splinters. The window set in the door was also broken. Jesse recognized Rodgers from a DARE presentation he'd given at his granddaughter's school. Family had been invited to attend the presentation, which had taken place in the gym. There had been Entenmann's coffee cake and coffee served afterword.

"Are you okay sir?" Rodgers said.

"Just shook as hell. Did you see it?"

"What did you see?"

"Well, it was a goddamned Bigfoot, if I'm being honest."

"Tell me what happened. Looks like your intruder cut itself," Rodgers said, pointing to blood on the area rug near the door.

Jesse filled in Rodgers, starting with Rosco barking and seeing the creature out in the woods. Then how it came near the house and he beat it upstairs.

"You didn't see it do any of this damage?"

"I was hunkered down in the attic. You believe me, right?"

"I do. Definitely don't think you kicked down your own door. Did you see where it went?"

"Like I said, I was nearly crapping my pants up in the attic."

"Stay put and I'm going to have a look."

Rodgers headed out back. His dark uniform was a blur in the falling snow. Rosco, still at Jesse's side, whined and licked Jesse's hand. "It's okay, bud. It's gone for now."

Seven

Tracking a cryptid wasn't part of the job description when Rodgers had been hired by the Barker Police. He'd been on the job fifteen years, getting promoted to Lieutenant last year. He hadn't grown up here, but he quickly learned that people believed in the Barker Monster. It was church in this town.

Rodgers had gotten enough calls and complaints over the years to take the creature seriously. It had died down in the last five years, but sightings were on the rise. Plus, he had that crew of researchers to deal with.

He headed straight out the back door, slogging through the snow. As he got to the fence, he noticed the first track. It was partially covered by the snow, but there was no doubting what had made it. Sixteen, eighteen inches long. He took out his smartphone and snapped a few pictures.

One section of the chain link had been ripped open. Rodgers headed to the torn section of fence. The Fence rail had been twisted like a bendy straw. Something of considerable strength had ripped the fence apart.

He squinted at the tree line. The snow didn't make it easy to see. Barker had tens of thousands of acres of woods on its border. The woods eventually butted up to Thompson State Park.

His suspect could be anywhere out there. Rodgers wasn't about to head into the woods alone. He'd float the idea of a search party by Hartmann. The chief would be reluctant to send people looking for boogeymen. He wasn't a believer.

Rodgers headed back to the house.

"Well?" Jesse said, standing inside the doorway.

"Found a print. I'm not pursuing your intruder alone."

"Don't think it's ever done something like this."

"We had an incident with a doorknob being turned, but never a forced entry like this," Rodgers said.

"What are you going to do about it?"

"I'm going to try and convince the chief to get a search party together."

"You going to kill it?"

"Don't know, but safety's an issue. Imagine if it had come after you in the house."

"Don't really want to think about that," Jesse said.

"Do you have somewhere to stay until that door gets fixed?"

"I can stay at my son's place. Have to button this up with plywood until someone can fix the door."

"I'll file a report. Call us if you see anything. And I wouldn't linger here for now," Rodgers said.

Rodgers headed back to the patrol vehicle. He placed the shotgun back in its mount and radioed his findings back to the station. He hoped Pinkowski wouldn't hang around for long. Once that opening was buttoned up, he needed to get gone.

Jesse examined the door. The window was smashed out. The wood had been splintered, and one hinge had been popped out and bent. It was hanging onto the frame for dear life. Twenty years ago, running to Home Depot solo and grabbing plywood wouldn't have been a big deal for him. He had the know-how to get the door buttoned up. Seventy-five was far removed from his fifties.

He'd have to call Tim for help.

Jesse had a few tarps in the basement. He needed something to at least keep the snow from blowing in. He headed down to the basement. Rosco stayed at the top of the stairs and whined.

"You're fine. I'll be right up," Jesse called.

The dog barked, as if telling Jesse to hurry up.

He grabbed the tarp and his staple gun. Had a small work bench and pegboard set up in one corner of the basement. Once upstairs, Rosco greeted him with an enthusiastic bark. "I know, you missed me, you goofball."

Jesse got the tarp stapled up outside the door frame. At least the snow wouldn't come whipping in. When the tarp was hung, he called Tim.

"What's up Dad?"

"What're you up to?"

"Got the day off. Was going to make a grocery run."

"I need your help."

"What's up?" Tim said.

This would be a fun one to explain. "Well, I'll just come out and say it. The damned Barker monster busted down the back door. Had the cops here."

"You serious?"

"No, it's a prank. I'm going to put it on You Tube."

"Okay, okay. When did this happen?"

"About half-an-hour ago. Police just left. I need help getting this door closed up."

"You safe?"

"For now. I took Rosco and hid up in the attic."

"And you saw it?"

"Rosco started going nuts. Had him outside. It came out of the woods and right up to the house. Smashed the door pretty good."

Tim exhaled. "Damn. Yeah, I'll be right over. Thinking we put some plywood over it for now?"

"That's my thought. You mind having a house guest until the door gets fixed?"

"I guess I can put up with an old man," Tim said with a laugh.

"Well you got no choice. I've got a reservation."

"I'll head out now."

The cold wind flapped the tarp. Jesse was freezing his ass off. He wanted to stay near the rear window in case his visitor decided to come back. Chilled, he grabbed a knit hat off a hook near the door. He also slipped on a pair of gloves.

Fifteen minutes later, he heard a truck engine in the driveway. He looked out and saw Tim's F-150. He put the leash on Rosco. No way he was leaving the dog here. Not with that thing out there and the door wide open.

He hoped it wouldn't come back while he was gone. Especially with nothing but plywood covering the doorway.

Jesse took Rosco out with him and put him in the rear of the cab. Rosco poked his head between the front seats and Tim scratched him on the head.

"Let's make this quick," Jesse said.

"You doing okay?"

"Shook up, but fine, yeah,"

Tim backed out and they headed to the Home Depot outside of Barker. A few more inches of snow had accumulated in the lot.

"I'll run in and get the plywood and screws," Tim said. "Wait here with Rosco."

"I can help."

"I'll throw it on a cart and bring it out. You can help me load it," Tim said.

That was fine with Jesse. He never left Rosco alone in the car and was glad to stay with the dog. Jesse headed inside, and fifteen minutes later, he came back with a sheet of plywood on a flat cart. Jesse hopped out, and the two of them loaded the plywood into the truck. Tim threw the box of screws in the cab and they drove back to Jesse's place.

The two of them sat in the truck and watched the house. Jesse didn't see or hear any signs of the creature. It wouldn't be so subtle as to lie in ambush for them. At least he hoped not. "Well, door isn't getting fixed sitting here."

"You ready?"

"Let's go."

They hopped out, leaving Rosco in the cab. He and Tim muscled the sheet of plywood into the house, Tim banging his elbow on the door frame and muttering *sonofabitch*. Once the plywood was set down, Jesse went out and brought Rosco inside.

"I'll grab the drill," Jesse said, and headed down to the basement. He grabbed the cordless drill, pulled the trigger, and revved it a few times.

Back upstairs, Tim was aligning the plywood over the doorway. He had the tarp down, but Jesse would want to tack that up over the wood as added protection.

It took about ten minutes to remove the door and tack the plywood up. Jesse then grabbed his staple gun and tacked the tarp up around the wood, covering any gaps. They set the door in the dining room.

"I noticed the blood," Tim said.

"It must've cut itself smashing the window."

"I guess the stories are true."

"I saw what I saw. No doubting it."

"Didn't grandpa see something one time?"

The story had been kept quiet in the family, but his father had quite the experience while camping. Had it written in an old, leather-bound journal. Jesse had never told Tim the story. Maybe someday he would. "He heard some strange noises. That was the end of it."

"Mom told me he wouldn't go back in the woods."

Jesse waved Tim off. "Your grandfather wasn't afraid of anything. Let me round up my stuff."

"I can get Rosco's stuff. Dog food in the pantry?"

"Yeah, his bowls are in the back room."

Jesse headed to the bedroom, where he had a suitcase under the bed. Hadn't used it since he and Ella had gone to the Dominican ten years ago. That had been a great time. They didn't do much more than sit on the beach, but that had been enough for Jesse. Just being with her was enough. Those days were gone, though.

He packed his clothes and toiletries in the suitcase. Packed enough for a week. Along with the clothes, he took his father's journal, which had been stashed in the top dresser drawer. When he went downstairs, Tim was waiting with Rosco on the leash. Rosco barked, as if telling him to get a move on.

"Hopefully this will be good for now," Jesse said.

"I'll get Teri over here to have a look. She owes me a favor."

"The sooner, the better."

"Re-hanging a door shouldn't be a problem."

"I want something solid."

Not that it would help much. He had a feeling that thing could smash through a steel door like it was paper.

"I'll call Teri right away."

Teri was good. From plumbing to carpentry to drywall, she could do everything. At least his new door would be hung properly. "We should warn her."

"Absolutely," Tim said. "Ready? Maybe it's just me, but I'm getting the creeps."

"It's not just you."

Monique nearly jumped off the bed when James finally came through the door. He'd walked down the street to a diner for breakfast. She was never one for a large breakfast, but James lived for waffles, pancakes, and eggs. She'd been happy with a cup of coffee from the room's K-Cup machine for now.

"Took you long enough," she said.

James slipped out of his coat. "You look like a kid on Christmas morning."

"I had the police scanner going. There was a sighting."

"Really?" James said, eyes getting wide.

She had the police scanner sitting on a table. There'd been a call where an officer responded to a large intruder outside a home. "Cops responded to a large, man-like intruder at a house. I wrote the address down."

"Think it's our guy?"

"What else would it be?"

"We should go out there, see if someone will talk to us."

"Is Kurt up?"

"Yeah. He went to grab the motel's continental breakfast."

"Let's round him up and go."

She would hold off on showering until tonight. Didn't want to waste daylight. Her belly rumbled and she grabbed a protein bar from her bag. After wolfing it down, she brushed her teeth and grabbed her bag. They had another scanner in the truck, which would allow them to track activity.

Monique couldn't wait to tell her dad about this. Unlike James' father, her dad had taken an interest in her research. She'd been fascinated with Bigfoot ever since watching *The Legend of Boggy Creek.* The grainy, pseudo-documentary that chronicled the Fouke Monster, had scared the hell out of her as a kid. She'd caught it on late-night cable.

It seemed a little cheesy now, but the terror she'd felt when the Fouke monster reached through a homeowner's window chilled her. She'd been hooked. Her and James had joined the team a few years ago after doing scut work and proving themselves on a few expeditions.

They headed out and knocked on Kurt's room door. Kurt answered. He had a blue do-rag wrapped around his dome. His long, graying beard glistened with beard oil. "About time. You two ready or are we going to sit around all day?"

"We're just waiting on your grumpy ass," Monique said. "We have a possible sighting. At a residence."

Kurt nodded his approval. "Nice. Let's roll."

"Are you carrying?" James said.

"Affirmative."

They headed out to the SUV. James got behind the wheel. Monique punched the address into the Maps app on her phone. Kurt piled in the back, grunting as he shifted in the seat. "Sure, make the old guy sit in back."

"I'm navigating," Monique said. "Gotta sit up front."

They headed five miles out of town, where the roads were flanked by dense forest. The GPS indicated the driveway was on the right. James turned and steered down the long drive. At the end was a two-story house done in red cedar shakes. A two-car garage stood to one side. No cars were parked in the driveway.

James turned up the windshield wipers to combat the increasing snowfall.

"Weather isn't helping," Kurt said.

"Just have to deal with it," James said.

"Doesn't look like anyone's home," Monique said. "I'll go knock."

"I can go if you want," Kurt said.

"We don't want them thinking we're here to rob the place."

"That's a low blow," Kurt said.

Monique got out and went to the front door. She rang the bell and heard it ding inside. Waited a few moments and knocked. No one answered. She inspected the windows and peeked inside. The house was dark, but she could see through to the back door, which was covered by plywood.

Back at the truck, James rolled down the window.

"The back door is covered in plywood," Monique said. "I'm having a look."

"What if they see you?"

"No one answered. I'll be right back."

"Hang on," James said. "Coming with."

James followed Monique around the house. A four-foot chain link fence surrounded the yard. One section of the fence had been destroyed. The fence rail had been bent.

"Wonder what did that?" James said.

Monique passed through the gate and approached the door. From this side, a blue tarp covered the plywood. The wind ripped, flapping the fabric.

Monique looked around, feeling like someone might be watching. She took out her phone and got a pic of the damaged door.

"Too bad no one's home," James said. "I'd love to hear the story."

Monique turned and looked at the woods. There was fifty yards of ground from the fence to the trees. She couldn't see well through the blowing snow. Did something shift between trees?

"Did you see something?" Monique said.

"Where?"

"Look at the woods," Monique said.

James peered beyond the fence, squinting. The snow dipped and whirled. Now she couldn't be sure she saw anything.

"I don't see anything."

They both peered at the woods for a few more moments. Nothing moved. It was getting tougher to see in the snow. A low roar cut through the whipping wind. Monique put a hand on James' arm and squeezed.

She fished a digital recorder from her pocket. Hit record. The roar came from the woods again. Something didn't want them around, and it sounded large.

"Did you get that?" James said.

"We'll see. Wind might make it tough."

"We should get back. Kurt has the gun."

A loud crack came from the woods. A small pine tree fell over, landing in the clearing. That was their cue to get going. This was amazing. Before this, the only thing she'd experienced was some far-off vocalizations. They were on to something here. Something big.

"I'm going to get a shot of it," Monique said.

"Don't be crazy."

"Watch yourself."

She slipped through the hole in the fence and went about halfway to the woods. A low growl came from the woods. "C'mon, show yourself."

From behind her, James muttered something. She turned and saw him on his phone. Probably calling Kurt. She held up her phone, wishing she'd brought their video camera. Phone video would have to do.

The downed tree was pulled back into the woods. Through the snow, she got a glimpse of movement, then the tree flew from the woods, heading in her direction. She stepped aside as it thudded nearby. It was a decent-sized trunk. Something incredibly strong would've thrown it.

"Back up, Mon," James said.

"Give me a second."

"What's going on?" Kurt said.

Monique glanced at Kurt. He his .44 with a long barrel in a holster, and she was glad for it.

"It just threw a damn tree," James said.

"And I got it on video."

James and Kurt joined Monique. Kurt kept his hand on the revolver's handle.

"It tore up this house, huh?" Kurt said.

"Looks that way," James said.

The unseen thing bellowed, a roar that she felt in her gut. Now it was time to get going. If something came charging out of those woods, they might not get be able to run. "I've got enough for now."

They retreated to the truck. She couldn't wait to send this back to the organization. This was huge.

"Did you actually see it?" Kurt said.

"No, but you heard that. And I got the tree throwing on video."

"I wouldn't want to be the one living in that house," James said.

"Maybe they won't be back," Monique said.

"I sure as hell wouldn't be," Kurt said.

James started up the truck and backed out of the driveway.

Jesse got settled in the spare room at Tim's house. Put his clothes in the dresser and arranged his deodorant, toothpaste, and toothbrush on the dresser. He also had some pain cream for his aching shoulder, stuff that smelled like Wintergreen Lifesavers. It worked pretty good, though, calming the steady ache down to a dull throb. He had tucked Dad's journal under his flannel shirts.

No reason to think Tim would go snooping, but better to be safe. It had been years since he'd cracked open the journal. Later on, when the house was quiet, he'd read some before bed.

"Hey Jesse, do you want anything?" Brian said,appearing in the doorway.

"How many times have I told you to call me Dad?"

"Right, Dad."

"You've officially been my son-in-law for two years. Enough with the Jesse crap."

"Got it Dad. Can I get you something to eat or drink?"

Brian wore a loose hoodie and plaid pajama pants. Thick socks on his feet. Both Tim and Brian worked from home. They had good-paying tech jobs. How the world had changed since Jesse was in the working world. He'd hauled his ass into a bus garage for thirty years, fixing diesel engines for the Niagara Frontier Transit Authority. The world had gone remote. "I'm good Brian, thanks."

"Fresh sheets on the bed. We're glad you're here."

"Well thanks for having me. Glad to be here."

"Tim said it was pretty bad."

"I thought it might be my last day on Earth. Was shaking up in that attic."

"Did you actually see it?"

"I did. Came right at the house."

Brian shuddered. "I never believed until I moved here and met Tim. Heard the howls. We get them from time-to-time around the house."

"It ain't no joke."

"I'm making burgers for dinner tonight. How do you like yours?"

"Just a touch pink."

"You've got it."

Brian left the room. He was a great guy and Jesse was happy for Tim and Brian. When Tim had come out in high school, the family had still been church goers. Upon the news getting out, Pastor Ted had asked Jesse to meet with him in private. The pastor, with his Abe Lincoln beard and shock of silver hair, informed Jesse that the congregation was upset about Tim.

"Why should they be?"

"Well, it's not God's will. Some say it's unnatural."

"And what do you say?"

"I don't condone it. Love the sinner, not the sin. I'm not sure how things will go for Tim here."

At that point, Jesse stood up, smoothed his shirt, and said, "Don't ever talk about my son like that again. And you can keep your church and your stupid damned beard." Jesse walked out, leaving the Pastor open-mouthed. Jesse hadn't been to a church since. Ella had agreed, referring in private to the congregation as "Narrow minded assholes." It was the only time he'd heard her use such language.

Tim and Brian had met at college. Brian was a transplant from rural Indiana. He'd left his family behind. They were about as open-minded as the church had been. Brian's parents had recommended conversation therapy. Brian had been assaulted by some guys outside a bar. The cops hadn't done shit. Hadn't helped that the guy who busted Brian's nose was the chief's brother-in-law. Brian hadn't talked to his family in ten years.

How anyone could shun their own child was beyond him. Jesse had lost a few friends and was currently at war with some family over Tim's marriage. His brother Nathan refused to attend the ceremony. Nathan currently sat at number one on Jesse's shit list. He didn't intend on being on friendly terms with anyone who didn't love and accept Tim.

Screw 'em in the ear, as his grandfather had been fond of saying when annoyed.

He was glad to have them both. They would put up with an old man for a few days while the door got fixed.

Jesse felt like a nap was in order. A weariness had settled into his muscles after the morning's events.

He kicked off his slippers and lay on the bed. That's when Tim came in with Rosco in tow. The dog hopped on the bed and curled up at Jesse's feet.

"Don't you know you shouldn't mess with a man's nap?"

"I won't keep you. Teri can stop out tomorrow to look at the door."

"Don't suppose I can get the insurance to pay for monster damage."

"That might be a tough sell."

"Figured we could get lunch and then meet her. She'll be there around one."

"Sounds like a plan."

He didn't want to go back to his house. Felt like a coward for feeling that way, and he'd never admit that to Tim. He felt right at home in the guys' spare room. Maybe they'd let him stay until this all blew over.

"Proceed with your nap," Tim said. "You want me to take furball with me?"

"He's fine. He'll sleep if I do."

"All right. Let us know if you need anything."

"I can get it. I'm not that feeble yet."

"I realize that. Just checking."

Jesse closed his eyes and folded his hands on his chest. Tim got the message and vacated the room.

Eight

Gina and the others had pancakes for breakfast. Outside, the snow continued to beat down. Six more inches had piled up overnight. Their plan to do some target shooting was thwarted for now. Probably couldn't even see to shoot out there. She'd called the restaurant just to check in. They had a great Friday night, again. It had been so crazy on Fridays they'd brought on two more servers and an extra bartender.

She was sitting at the kitchen table sipping some coffee when Steve joined her. He pulled out a chair and sat down.

"It was quiet last night."

"Those noises stopped, yeah," Gina said.

"I was thinking of taking a look around," he said.

"In this?"

"It's just a little snow."

"You sure that's a good idea?"

"We're armed. Wanna join me?"

She wanted to sit here and sip coffee, then retreat to the couch with her book and sit in front of the fire.

"Hear me out," he said.

"Okay, I'm listening."

"I'd just like to know how close it might have come to the cabin."

"You a monster hunter now?"

"What if it was skulking around last night?"

"That's you, babe, always curious."

"I'm serious. We'll take the guns and just have a look outside."

"Now I'm in on this?" Gina said.

"You're my ride or die, babe."

That got a laugh out of Gina. "And you're mine. All right. I'll indulge you. But we're not going frolicking in the woods."

"Frolicking?"

"It's all I got. Let me finish my coffee and we'll have a look."

Her coffee finished, Gina went up to the bedroom and changed into jeans and a heavy sweater. She'd had on pajama pants and a sweatshirt. They'd brought the concealed carry holster for the semi-automatic, and she strapped it on. Steve would be carrying the shotgun.

David and Priya's door was closed. They'd gone back upstairs after breakfast. No need to disturb them.

Down by the front door, Gina and Steve put on their winter gear, then stepped outside. She forced the door closed against the wind. David and Priya's Jeep was a white lump in the snow.

They hadn't thought to ask about driveway plowing. Even with four-wheel-drive, it might be tough getting out. She supposed they'd worry about that later.

"All right, big time hunter, where do you want to start?" she asked.

"I want to have a look around the perimeter, then check the deck."

They trekked along the side of the garage. She peered in the garage window, where two motorcycles under tarps, a Mercedes, and a pick-up were parked. Too bad there was no room for the Jeep. It would've saved them digging out.

Nothing notable along the side of the garage. They rounded the back of the garage, where the property sloped upward to the woods. The large deck, built on high posts, was to the right.

Gina looked up at the bathroom window, out which she'd seen something lurking in the trees. Had it been watching her the whole time? Maybe waiting for an opportunity to approach the house? That thought made her skin feel like beetles were dancing on it.

Steve and Gina passed the deck and headed to the other side of the lodge. They stayed close to the structure, and when they came to one of the windows, Gina noticed something. Underneath the window, snagged in between logs, was a tuft of thick, black fur. Steve was slightly ahead, and she tapped him on the shoulder.

As he turned, Gina said, "Check this out. It's fur."

Steve inspected the fur, then plucked it between his fingers. "It's been near the house."

"That could've been there a while," Gina said.

"Or it could be from last night. No way to tell."

"That's damned creepy. What if it was right outside while we were sleeping?"

"We need to tell Priya and David."

She felt uneasy being out here. The blowing snow obscured the view of the woods, which were dark to begin with. Something could be watching them right now. "We should head back inside."

"No argument there," Steve said. "Let's just check out the deck."

"Agreed, then we head inside."

They headed up the steps onto the deck. Trudging through the snow, they came to the French doors. Gina inspected them. No sign of anything trying to get in, and no fur left behind. This was turning out to be stressful. And it was supposed to be a vacation.

The French doors swung out, and were blocked by snow, so they'd have to go around. She and Steve returned to the front door and shook the snow off themselves. Gina had the bit of fur in her pocket.

After stepping inside, they got out of their winter gear and set their boots on the trays near the door. Priya came downstairs, followed by David. They were both dressed in white robes, like they just came from the spa. Priya's dark hair was damp.

"Went for a hike?" Priya asked.

"Did you shoot something for dinner?" David said, seeing the shotgun.

"No, but we found something odd," Gina said.

Priya paused at the bottom of the stairs, and David bumped into her.

"Piece of fur stuck to the side of the cabin. Near the window," Steve said.

"I have it here," Gina said, and took it from her pocket. She held it up. Priya came closer and inspected it.

"Something got close then," Priya said.

David came and had a look at the fur. "Wonder if it could be analyzed? I'd be curious."

"Everyone should stay close to the house," Gina said. "Although I don't think we're going to be going far in this storm."

"The Jeep is buried," Steve said.

"I'll dig it out after I get dressed," David said.

"I'll give you a hand," Steve said.

Gina headed to the kitchen, where she took out a box of quart-sized plastic storage bags. She ripped one from the box and put the fur inside. Then she sealed it up and put it in a drawer. "I think we should call someone, report what we've seen."

"I don't think that's a bad idea, just in case," Priya said.

Both David and Steve agreed.

Steve said, "So who's the lucky one going to make the call?"

"I will," Gina said.

Roland stared at the phone. It was gray, with a digital display and a ton of buttons. He imagined you'd find one like in office buildings all around the country. The Hope Center kept it in a small room on a table. There was a plastic chair. The door could be closed for privacy. A sign, printed on copy paper, was taped to the wall: *Please be considerate. Keep calls under ten minutes.*

He didn't have many occasions to make calls. The last time he'd talked to Alex, it had been in this room. Now, he had a chance at getting off the road. Off the streets. This should be a good thing. Why was he so damned nervous, then?

He picked up and dialed Alex's number. It was Alex's direct line at work. Maybe he'd be away from his desk. Alex answered on the third ring.

"Hey, it's me," Roland said.

"Roland? Jesus, how are you?"

"I'm staying at the Hope Center in Barker."

"You good? You safe and warm? Weather is shit."

"It's gotten worse today. But I've got three hots and a cot, as they say," Roland said.

"So what's going on?"

"I was thinking about your offer."

"And?"

"What would I be doing?"

"The job? You'd be starting in our warehouse. Pulling shipping orders, loading trucks. Eventually we could get you trained on the forklift. This is so great," Alex said.

"I'll need a ride up there, and a place to stay."

"You're staying with me, no arguments."

"I won't argue."

Alex lived about forty-five minutes from Barker. It would take longer to get here in this weather. "You okay giving me a ride?"

"Well how else you getting here? I'm not putting my brother on a bus."

"As long as you don't mind the drive."

"I'll cut out of work a little early. I've got a ton of hours in this week, anyway. Boss won't mind if I cut out early."

"All right. See you later."

"It'll be around four. Hey, Roland, I'm glad you're doing this."

"Yeah, me too."

They said their goodbyes and Roland hung up the phone. He found his hands were trembling. He'd dropped out so long ago. The return to normal life would be odd. Getting up for work. Having a steady roof over his head and not eating shelter sandwiches and soup. He would pay Alex rent. No living for free. Roland would insist on it, and Alex would refuse. Then they'd do this dance like when people dicker over who's picking up the bill for dinner.

He'd make Alex take the money. Even homeless, Roland had made money doing odd jobs here and there. Shoveling snow. Mowing lawns and raking for people. He only resorted to panhandling if he was desperate, and even then, it made him feel somehow greasy. Plus, the looks he got from some people were intended to kill.

He wasn't some damned rat or cockroach. Just a guy who hit the skids. A guy who liked to play guitar and cook in his old life. Someone who was just like them. Most people didn't realize how thin the line was between someone like Roland and themselves.

They were only a house fire or a health crisis away from the streets. Maybe if they realized that, some people wouldn't look at him like he was dog crap.

He headed back to his cot, feeling like he was floating. Moments of good fortune had been few. This was a good day. A chance at something new. Part of him worried that it would melt away, like Alex would call and rescind the offer.

He'd feel better once he was at his brother's house. It would seem more real, then. No takebacks, as they used to say as kids.

Gina heard an engine cut out, and she looked out to see a police SUV parked behind Steve and Priya's vehicle. An officer got out and trudged through the snow. She moved away from the window, as not to stare. A moment later, he knocked on the door, and Gina opened it.

Snow dusted the big cop's jacket and hat.

"We got a call about an animal."

"I'm the one who called. Come in."

The officer came in and shut the door. The name badge on his jacket read *Rodgers*. Rodgers stomped his feet on the entry mat and snow crumbled off his boots.

Priya called from the kitchen: "Would you like some coffee?"

"I appreciate it, but no thanks. Tell me what happened."

"It started last night. I saw something out the bathroom window."

David said, "And don't forget about after the accident."

"Start with last night. What did you see?"

"We heard screams and howls. I looked down and something big was standing near the trees."

"Can you describe it?"

"Big. On two legs. Covered in fur."

Rodgers nodded. "Where did it go from there?"

"I don't know. I ran downstairs. We didn't see it again after that."

"But we heard noises," Steve said.

"And what about the accident?"

Priya and David took turns recounting the deer, running off the road, the deer's head, and David hearing something large and animal-like.

"The deer's head was severed, you say," Rodgers said.

"Yeah. Like I said, it smacked the back window of our vehicle," David said.

Rodgers was silent for a moment. Gina couldn't read him, as his face was impassive. "Do you have guns?"

"We do," Gina said. "We have pistol permits if you want to see them."

"Not necessary. I'd recommend keeping your firearms handy," Rodgers said. "If you choose to stay."

"What exactly is going on, officer?" Priya asked.

"I'll be blunt. This is a hotbed for Bigfoot activity. Look up the Barker Monster. I'd like to say it's just a legend, but I'd be wrong."

"Is it dangerous?" Gina asked.

"It's known to be aggressive. Sightings started up again a few months ago. I wouldn't go wandering if you stick around. Is there anything else I can help with?"

Priya grabbed the bag with the fur sample in it and brought it over. She handed it to Rodgers, who held it up to the light and examined it. "Mind if I take this?"

"We don't mind," David said.

Priya slid off the stool at the breakfast bar. "Are you doing anything to track it down?"

"In the process. Whether or not we put together a hunting party is up to our police chief. Call us if you see anything else."

With that, Rodgers adjusted his hat and headed out the door. Snow blew in while the door was open and dusted the welcome rug.

"We're not going anywhere in this weather," David said.

"Looks like we're stuck inside," Gina said. "We need to make sure the place is locked up."

"Not a problem. I don't see what that thing would want with us, anyway," David.

Gina didn't want to think about that. It had an interest in the house. The thing wouldn't have been standing outside, otherwise. Maybe they were encroaching on its territory. Hopefully the past day's events would be isolated incidents. The police would handle things, wouldn't they?

Jesse awoke from his nap and headed downstairs to the kitchen. A cup of coffee was in order. Tim was in the office off the living room. Brian was typing on his laptop at the dining room table.

He found some K-Cups in the drawer. Popped one in the coffee maker and let it brew. The rich aroma of a dark roast filled the kitchen. He grabbed his cup of coffee and headed back to the bedroom, where he planned on reading some of Dad's journal.

First, he shut the door. After he set his coffee on the nightstand, he pulled the journal from the drawer like he was a burglar stealing jewels. It wasn't like Tim suspected he had a secret journal, but he felt the need to be caution.

Jesse propped up some pillows and lay on the bed. Then he flipped the journal open. The pages were yellowed and still smelled faintly of the cigars his dad favored. Mom had hated them, and Dad resorted to smoking them in the garage.

The first page contained his Dad's name in scratchy handwriting: *Henry Pinkowski. 1959-1960.*

He turned the page and skimmed it before diving in. The first entry was from September of 1959. Jesse had been in the fourth grade at Truman Elementary. He'd had a crush on Jill Masterson, who had the prettiest red hair you'd ever seen. That was before they started calling them gingers and claiming redheads had no soul. Shame, really. He'd always liked red hair.

Jesse went to the first entry. The start of Dad's camping trip at the state park.

September 7, 1959

I found a good spot after hiking in three or four miles. Nice clearing with a lot of downed wood for a fire. I parked the wagon in the park's lot. Should be fine for a few days. I can hear the stream not far from here. Not much wildlife around, but I'm sure I'll see some soon.

I'll set the tent up and get camp going. Then maybe sneak in a little fishing before supper. This trip is going to be good for me. The back is still tight, but I'm moving around good enough. Should be back at the plant in a few weeks. Thank God for Maria. She's been picking up extra hours at the bakery and doing some seamstress work on the side.

We should be okay, but I want to get back to work. It was her idea for me to head out here. Get some fresh air and heal after the accident. Damned stupid thing. That idiot that bumped the ladder got fired. Served him right. He was half drunk most of the time, anyway.

Time for some fishing.

I got a couple small trout. It was still down by the lake. A couple times I thought I saw someone standing on the other side of the lake. Just out of sight in the woods. Suppose it could've been a hiker. Stood there for a good, long while, though. I'm going to cook these trout up, eat, and watch the sunset.

He remembered how his father had returned from the trip. Upon coming home, he'd thrown his gear in the garage and slammed the door. That was unusual. Dad always had spots for everything. Every tool was on a pegboard. Screws and nails went in mason jars and coffee cans. Fishing poles were hung on the garage walls. His father had gone straight up to his room and closed the door after throwing the gear in the garage.

He'd stayed up there for hours, even when his mother had knocked on the door multiple times. Took dinner in his room, something he never did. After that day, he never spoke of the camping trip again. His mother warned Jesse not to ask about it. All she would say was something spooked Dad in those woods and he wasn't to ask about it.

He'd come to learn what had happened upon reading the journal. It'd been six months after Dad died when Jesse had found the journal. The truth had come out. His mother had suffered the indignities of Dementia, so he couldn't ask her about Dad's journal. At the time, she'd been in a secure unit at Falling Waters Elder Care. He saw her once a week, and she didn't recognize him anymore. Called him Roger, who was his cousin.

He would bring Mom flowers every week. One time, after setting the vase on her dresser, she said, "What the fuck are those, you cunt?" So much for the flowers. His mother – who never uttered anything stronger than darn – had sworn at him like a sailor.

He was getting tired reading, so he went downstairs to see how Tim was making out with his contractor friend. He found Tim in the kitchen boiling some water for tea.

"Did you touch base with Teri?"

"I did. She can meet us tomorrow around two."

"She's reasonable?"

"Fair as can be."

"All right. I don't' want to get screwed. What did you tell her?"

"Some animal busted your door," Tim said.

"Good an explanation as any."

"She's from Barker. She'll have questions."

"If she asks, I'll give honest answers."

Nine

Monique's phone rang and the number popping up belonged to Doctor Burrell. She'd emailed him the footage of the snapped tree and the vocalizations. She answered.

"Monique, this is amazing."

"Isn't it?"

"Did you get confirmation that it attacked the house?"

She had detailed in her email what they'd found at the house and the police chatter they'd heard on the scanner. "It apparently ripped the door off."

"Did you see any prints?"

"It was snowing too hard. Anything would've been covered up."

"We've got to get into the field. I'm coming out there with a few other team members."

She wanted this for her and James alone. They'd done the grunt work, getting footage and risking their safety. Burrell was a decent guy, but he'd swoop in and take things over. But he was the boss and he had the degree. There was no way to stop him from coming here.

"Have you talked to anyone else? Police?"

"They paid us a visit when we got in. Told us to be careful and not to trespass."

"We won't talk about how you got the video."

"No one saw us. I think the homeowner vacated."

"It ripped the door right off," Burrell said, sounding impressed. "A documented attack on a home. It must be unusually aggressive."

"That's why we brought guns."

"Those are a last resort."

"Of course they are. But you saw that video. No one should go out there unarmed."

"Understood. But remember, we're researchers first."

If Burrell heard those howls up close, he might change his mind. She wasn't deterred, but she was glad they had the guns with them. "When are you coming? The weather's bad."

"We'll get there as soon as we can."

"Snow's gonna slow you down."

"What's next for you and James? Interviews?"

"I'd love to talk to the homeowner," Monique said. "We have a few others. Credible people who've reported sightings."

"What about the guy who had his doorknob turned?"

Monique scrolled through her notes. "Casey Webster. That's our doorknob guy. I'd love to hear from him."

Burrell said he'd see them soon and ended the call. Monique put the address with the busted door into Google. The owner's name was Jesse Pinkowski. She searched for other Pinkowskis in the area. There was a Timothy Pinkowski living nearby. That wasn't a common name. Might be some relation.

James had been checking out the vending machines. He returned with a bag of extra-hot chips and a Coke. "What's up?"

"Burrell was impressed. He's heading out here."

"Can't wait. This was our gig," James said.

"Had to expect that after what we sent him."

"We do the shit work and he gets the glory."

James sat on the bed and ripped open his bag of chips.

"You always eat alone?" Monique said.

He held out the bag, offering her a chip. She took one. They were covered in dark red powder. She ate it, and immediately regretted it. It was hotter than the devil's ass crack. "Hand me that pop."

He gave it over and she took a swig, cooling her mouth and throat. "There's something wrong with you if you eat those."

"Can't get enough of 'em."

"I pity your insides tomorrow morning. We've still got some daylight. Wanna do some interviews?"

"Yeah, where do you want to start?"

"This Casey guy. The one who had his door opened."

"From what I read about him, he seems to like the attention. Been interviewed before."

"Should be interesting," Monique said.

Dale Cheevers was having a hell of a time seeing. The snow came down like a bitch, and his wipers weren't keeping up. His circular saw had taken a crap, and his extra was at one of the other houses he was working on. He'd texted the homeowner, who'd left him a key, announcing he was picking up his saw.

Dale didn't need to text, but he felt better letting the customer know he was in the house. Even with having a key. He turned up the driveway and parked in the driveway. While he was here, he'd check on the kitchen. One of his guys had started tiling the floor, and he wanted to have a look.

He hopped out of the truck and headed to the front door. Once inside, he slipped his boots off and proceeded to the kitchen. It had been a total gut job. The floor looked good, so far, and Dale was happy with the progress.

His circular saw was in the attached garage. The longer he stayed here, the more time he lost at the other job. He entered the garage, where his circular saw rested in a plastic case. Dale also had a portable table saw and a bucket with electrical tools in it stashed here.

When he went to pick up the saw, something passed the window. Something dark that momentarily blocked the gray light filtering in the garage. Dale stood up. He heard crunching snow outside. Footsteps. Someone was outside and moving along the perimeter of the house.

He crept to the window. Outside was a curtain of snow. Couldn't see a damn thing out there. He'd pick up his saw and get out, call the cops if he must.

Dale picked up his saw case and headed into the kitchen. His back to the window, he became aware of someone watching him. He whipped around. A pair of large, red eyes glared at him. There, then gone. His heart rate shot up. Neck hair prickled.

"What the fuck?" he said.

He slipped into the adjacent dining room, where a sliding door led out to the patio. Dale peered outside. A huge, man-sized shape stepped to the doors. Dale couldn't see the head or face, just a massive frame covered in fur.

Either someone was screwing with him, or the legends around town were true. That son-of-a-bitch was seven feet tall if it was an inch. Dale backed into the kitchen. A deep grunt came from outside.

It wasn't far to the truck. He could hurry out the front door and be in the driveway. Just a matter of how fast the thing on the patio could move. Could it get around the house before he got in the truck?

Maybe he was safer in here. He considered calling the police. How was he going to report it, though? Something thudded against the glass. He looked around the corner and saw the thing testing the glass with its curled fist.

Just a matter of time if it wants to come in. There might not be time for the police to get here. He set down his saw case, figuring it would slow him down. Have to come back for it another time.

Dale bolted for the front door. Behind him, glass smashed. He fumbled with the deadbolt, aware of a pungent stink in the house. It thudded through the kitchen. He got the door unlocked. As he was about to open it, he was yanked backward and hit the living room floor, looking up.

The creature reached down and palmed his face. It squeezed. Dale felt the pressure build in his skull. He beat at the thing's arm, but the force intensified. Something cracked in his face, and searing pain shot through his skull.

The creature lifted Dale, palming his face like a basketball, then it slammed his head against the floor. His vision got hazy, and then he faded out.

Ten

Casey Webster greeted them at his front door. He wore a pair of dark jeans held up by suspenders and an old mechanic's shirt with the name *Frank* embroidered on it. Monique took him for about sixty. He had a few patches of white hair under his chin where he'd missed shaving.

"You the Bigfoot people?" he said.

"I'm the one who called, yes," Monique said.

Webster introduced himself, even though they'd chatted on the phone.

"Monique. This is James."

"Come in. Get out of that cold," Webster said.

He led them to a kitchen, with a huge slab of a table. Monique noted shelving high on the kitchen walls. On the shelving were a collection of beer steins and mugs.

"Like some tea or coffee?"

They both said no thanks, and all three of them sat at the kitchen table. "So you're Bigfoot people."

"That's right," James said. "Second largest group of Bigfoot researchers in the Northeast."

"Well I've talked to one other organization, plus the folks from Discovery Channel. They were out here making a documentary."

Monique hadn't seen that. They wouldn't be breaking any new ground with the interview, but she believed in being thorough. Plus, she really wanted to hear Webster's story firsthand. "Mind if I record this?"

"Go ahead."

She took out a digital recorder, set it on the table, and pressed record, noting the date, time, and the subject.

"Do you live by yourself?" Monique asked.

"Yep. Never married. Had the odd girlfriend, but mostly I like to be alone."

"Tell me what it's like living here," Monique said.

"Mostly quiet. Lots of deer coming around. They ate the hell out of my blackberry bushes. Nearest neighbors aren't in sight, which is how I like it, not that I'm unfriendly."

"Neighbors can be a pain," James said.

"Agreed. Guess I'm a bit of a hermit."

"What do you think about the Barker Monster?"

"Oh, I believe. Some don't, but I do."

"Tell me about the incident with your door."

"It was two years ago, roughly. I was sitting there watching the eleven o'clock news, eating popcorn and drinking a beer. That's when I hear someone on the back porch."

James said, "Did you get up to investigate?"

"I'm getting there. I figured it's raccoons trying to get at my trash, so I ignore it, but then it gets louder. Too loud to be a 'coon. Something's really banging around out there, so I get up and go to the back door."

"Did you see anything?"

"Not at first. I could see a shadow through the glass. It was blocking the spotlight I have on the deck. Then the doorknob turned. I don't usually lock the back door until bed, but that night I did, thank the Lord. I gave a yell. The knob turned a few times, then it gave up. When I looked out the window, I see it heading back to the woods."

"Can you describe it?"

"Giant. Broad shoulders. Hairy."

"Did it come back at all?"

Webster shook his head. "No, but I've heard it howling out there. I make sure the doors are locked. Got a rifle, too, if it comes back some night."

"Did it occur to you to move?" James asked.

"I've lived in this house for thirty-five years. Where would I go?"

Monique wanted to say just about anywhere an angry Sasquatch didn't live, but she stayed silent.

"Do you feel safe?" James asked.

"I didn't sleep well for a while, but then the howls stopped for a few years. Didn't hear anything, so it kind of faded from my mind, but I think it's back. I hear the sounds at night. My rifle isn't far away."

"Did you file a police report?"

"They're aware. What were they going to do? News people got wind of it and came to interview me. I shot my mouth off down at The Republic, which I shouldn't have done. Word spread."

"What'll you do if it comes back?" James said.

"Defend myself. Send it packing, hopefully."

Webster shifted in his seat, ran his thumbs up and down his suspenders.

"Were you always a believer?" Monique asked.

"Always. Too many people have seen it around to deny it. Then I had my own encounter, of course. You might want to follow up with a couple other people, too. I know of people who've seen it, and they'd be willing to tell their stories."

"I'd appreciate that."

He rattled off a list of names and addresses, then offered them a beverage one more time. They declined. Monique wanted to get a move on and talk to more people. Jesse Pinkowski was next on her list. Now there was a story.

Rodgers had made his way through the squad room, getting stopped multiple times for people to ask him about what happened at the Pinkowski house. He'd told it straight. Some of his fellow officers had sightings and stories of their own. He was on his way to have a meeting with the Chief about looking for the thing. Or at least coming up with a plan for securing the town and keeping watch.

"Rodgers? Ready for you."

Chief Cranston poked his head out from his office. He was up. He entered the office. Cranston's familiar model car was parked on his desk. A mint-green, late-fifties Chevy with tail fins. It resembled the two restored cars Cranston owned. He was fond of putting them in car shows, and the mint-green Chevy was his baby.

"I tell you we took home a ribbon at the last show of the year?" Cranston said.

"You did. The Chevy, right?"

"Of course. Anything new on that incident at the Pinkowski place?"

"Took a drive by and he's vacated, far as I can tell."

"Can't say I blame him."

"Some campers staying up on Seventy-Eight had a few incidents, too."

"What happened?"

Rodgers relayed the story about the deer's head and the sightings in the woods and by the lodge.

"Can't believe this shit's starting again."

"Chief, I know you're skeptical, but I brought back a hair sample," Rodgers said, pulling the plastic baggie from his pocket.

He handed it to Cranston, who held it up and examined it. "Where'd they find this?"

"Stuck to the side of the lodge, under the window."

Cranston turned the baggie around in his hands, then opened it. From his drawer, he took a pen and removed the fur. "Damn, that smells bad. Bear?"

"Don't know. I think it warrants having a look. Get a party together."

Cranston examined the fur for a moment longer before placing it back in the bag. He zipped it back up and handed it to Rodgers.

"I could see if the state boys will come out and help us," Rodgers said. "In the meantime, we'll step up patrols, especially by the Pinkowski place."

"I'm guessing word has spread. What about the people staying at that log home?"

"They plan on sticking around?"

"They didn't mention leaving," Rodgers said.

"I'd stop by and tell them it's at their own risk."

"Are you becoming a believer?"

"I believe in evidence. A busted door and multiple eyewitnesses are cause for concern. Organize extra patrols. I'll get overtime authorized if we need it," Rodgers said.

Part of him wanted to head into the woods out of curiosity. Another part of him would be happy to stay in his nice, warm patrol car and forget about monsters in the woods.

As Rodgers was nearing the end of his shift, he got a call. Dead body found out in the Applewood subdivision. He put the hammer down and sped out to the location. One of his guys was already on scene, Rex Anthony. Anthony stood near the front door. His skin looked ashen, and he'd hooked his thumbs in his beltloops. Trying to keep them from shaking.

"Hey Lieutenant."

"What'd you find?"

"White male, from what I can tell."

"From what you can tell?"

"He's in bad shape. His head was...crushed."

Had to keep calm, no matter how bad it got. Couldn't get rattled in front of the men. The worst scene he'd ever worked had been a dual MVA fatality. Jeep missed a turn and went head-on into a telephone pole. Vehicle burst into flames. When he arrived, the occupants were still alive and burning. Those screams and the odor of burned metal and scorched flesh were things he'd never forget.

They were looking for a missing man named Dale. He hadn't come home for dinner. Hadn't called his wife, either, and according to her, Dale always texted or called. They'd tracked him down to this house, where he was doing a kitchen renovation.

"Crime scene on the way?" Rodgers said.

"First thing I did."

"Good man," he said, clapping Anthony on the shoulder as he stepped inside.

The lights were on in the house, and the body was ten feet from the door. The skull had been crushed, and brains oozed from the ruined cranium. Bits of bone and brain matter had been crushed into the rug. The burning MVA victims were nothing compared to this.

Rodgers felt a breeze whip through the house. Careful to sidestep the gore on the carpet, he moved through the house. In the kitchen, the glass in the patio door had been smashed. Mud and water had been slopped on the tile floor.

Someone assaulted this Dale guy. Wanted to get at him bad enough to smash the door in. Rodgers drew his Glock and crept up to the door. He flipped on a light switch, and a spotlight lit up the patio. The blowing snow made visibility an issue.

He scanned the patio. No sign of prints. The snow would've covered any tracks. He had the homeowner's name and went out front to call the guy, one Harold Weever.

Rodgers dialed. Weever picked up on the third ring.

"Hello?"

"Mr. Weever? This is Lieutenant Rodgers with the Barker Police."

"Is everything okay?"

"Sir, we found a body in your house. We need to identify him. It appears he was assaulted."

Weever gasped. "How did this happen? Is it Dale? He was doing work at the house."

"We're not sure. We have to identify the body."

"What do I do? I'm out of town until next week Wednesday."

"You might want to come back. Your back door is also smashed in. The patio door."

"Goddammit. Dale was a good guy."

"We're unsure it was Dale, like I said."

"Just hope it's not him."

"Is this the best number for you, Mr. Weever? One of our detectives will follow up."

"Yeah, yeah. This is my cell."

"Someone will be in touch. You'll want to get that door buttoned up."

"I'll make some calls," Weever said.

"We'll be in touch."

Weever thanked him and ended the call. Rodgers turned to see the van from the crime lab pull into the driveway. This was going to be a goddamned messy one.

He watched the team head into the house, carrying their gear. Rodgers went in and watched them go to work. A few moments later, the county medical examiner arrived. Rodgers stood back while the ME looked over the body. Their detective also arrived on the scene and made a preliminary ID based on the guy's wallet. It was Dale Cheevers. The ME put the time of death at around 4-5 hours ago.

The cause of death was apparent: a squashed head. And he knew what had killed Cheevers. Some random psycho with a sledgehammer hadn't tracked the contractor to the house. They had something big and angry running around the woods.

Rodgers stepped outside. Two of the ME's people wheeled out the body in a bag and loaded it into the van. He didn't envy the person who had to do the autopsy on that mess.

Lisa Perez, their detective, stepped outside. She was tall, with dark, piercing eyes. She wore a wool coat, and as she approached, her badge swung from a lanyard hung around her neck.

"Bad one, huh Rodgers?" Perez said.

"Hope it was at least quick for the poor bastard."

"You know what the chatter is in there about what killed him, right?"

"I can imagine."

"Same thing supposedly broke down a door, right?"

Rodgers nodded. "I was out there earlier. Guy named Pinkowski. I'm trying to convince Cranston to let us go find it."

"Looking for the boogeyman?"

"You don't believe?"

"I'll believe it when I see it," Lopez said.

"Someone would have to be pretty pissed off at that guy to crush his skull like that."

"You'd be surprised."

"His wallet was intact?"

"It was. I just need to explore all options. Did you contact the homeowner?"

"He's out of town. I'll send you his number if you want. Told him a detective would follow up."

A gust of wind rocked the house. Lopez's overcoat flapped like a flag in the breeze, and her ponytail whipped around. Rodgers was glad to be mostly bald on days like this. Didn't have to worry about hair getting messed up. "If you've got this under control, I'm gonna head out."

"All good. Don't forget to send me that number."

As Rodgers headed back to his patrol vehicle, he took out his phone and texted Lopez the homeowner's contact info. He was glad this day was over. The kids were home alone, and he wanted to get back and check on them. At thirteen and sixteen, they were old enough to stay alone, but recent events had him worried.

He fought his way through the storm, getting across town and pulling in the driveway. Allie's beater Subaru was buried under the snow, parked in front of the garage. The spotlight shone down on it, and snowflakes danced in the yellowish light.

He parked behind the Subaru and fought his way through the wind to the house. Once inside, he took off his coat and hat. The light shined from the kitchen.

"You girls in there?" Rodgers said.

Allie called back, "No, someone broke in."

"Cut it out," Hannah said.

Hard to believe the girls were sixteen and thirteen. Allie driving. Hannah wanting to date a freshman from the high school. That request had gotten a hard no from Rodgers. It seemed like yesterday they were in dance recitals and school plays. Now they were teenagers, expert smartasses. Good kids, though. Did well in school. Never in trouble. He felt lucky.

Rodgers entered the kitchen. There was a lasagna on the counter and sliced Italian bread on a cutting board. Hannah had become quite the cook, taking after Skylar. She'd passed on her gift for cooking, among other things, to the girls. Dammit, he missed her. It had been three years since she found the lump under her arm.

The cancer had spread quickly. Liver. Lungs. Spine. He was a widower at forty-five years old. And the girls were without their mother. Fortunately, they were every bit as strong and smart as Skylar.

"There's lasagna," Hannah said.

Both girls had their laptops out. "Hope that's homework."

"Yes, Dad," they said in unison.

He grabbed a plate from the cupboard and served himself up lasagna and two slices of bread. Then he sat at the head of the table. "I need to talk to you both."

"What'd we do now?" Hannah said.

"Just listen. I don't want either of you going anywhere alone."

"What happened?" Allie said.

"Someone got killed over in the Applewood subdivision. It was a nasty one."

"Details?" Hannah said.

"No go," Rodgers said. "You know I can't tell you. Just worried about you."

"Will you catch the guy?" Hannah said, typing away at the keyboard.

"There was another incident earlier. Guy had his door smashed in. He was home at the time."

"Was he hurt?" Allie said.

"No, just scared him. The intruder left."

"Did you catch the guy?" Hannah said.

Here was the part that was going to sound ridiculous. "It wasn't a guy. You've heard the stories."

"Not the Barker Monster dad. Seriously?" Allie said.

"The man saw it himself, and I'd consider him credible."

Jesus, he felt like he was testifying in court.

"Maybe we should call the Bigfoot hunting show to film it," Hannah said.

"Yeah, mountain monster rednecks or whoever those guys are," Allie said.

"I'm serious. Look, either way, you two need to be careful."

"We're not going far with the snow, anyway," Hannah said.

Rodgers glanced out the kitchen window. It wasn't letting up. The kids might not have school Monday if this kept up. "When it stops snowing, I mean."

"We won't go lurking in the woods," Allie said.

"Or looking for Sasquatch," Hannah said.

"Teenagers. Can I send you both back for a refund?"

"Rodgers with a hilarious dad joke at the buzzer," Hannah said.

"Remember I pay for your phones and *your* car insurance," he said, digging at his lasagna.

"We'll be careful. Promise," Allie said.

"Famous last words," Rodgers said.

Eleven

Jesse was sitting in an armchair in the bedroom, tucked in the corner. A floor lamp next to the chair gave him plenty of reading light. He needed it more and more these days. That, and reading glasses. Trying to read small print was damned near impossible.

He had a fully belly and felt sleepy. Brian had made burgers with a bacon jam on them. Brian and Tim had shared a bottle of wine during dinner. Jesse declined the drink. He would've been in a coma if he had wine on top of a big burger.

Despite being tired, he flipped open Dad's journal, intent on reading some more. The entry continued. Same date. September 7th, 1959.

Back at camp now. Got the fish cooked over the fire. They were good. It's nice being out here. Quiet. Clear night and lots of stars overhead. This was a good idea. Need to clear my mind so I can get back to it. Back to work. I've felt useless since the injury. I know Maria doesn't think that, but I feel that way. I'd never tell her that, though. Might burn this thing after I finish writing.

When I came back to camp, I still had a funny feeling. When I walked away from the lake and looked back, I felt like someone was still watching. Still feel that way now, a little bit. Suppose it's just the odd feeling of being alone out in the woods. Most people wouldn't be keen on it, but it is peaceful.

I brought a book to read. A detective novel written before the War, when the pulps were booming. Think I'll settle in and read for a bit.

There was something near the camp. I read about twenty pages before I heard it. I threw some more logs on the fire. If it's good and bright, any animals should stay away. Definitely something large, maybe a black bear. It grunted, then walked off. Stank like nothing else, though. I'll keep the fire going for a while. Never thought to bring the shotgun. Wished I had it right now.

Jesse closed the journal, keeping his thumb in it to hold his place. He removed his reading glasses and rubbed his eyes. The entries about the trip took up the middle section of the journal. Most of the journal was mundane stuff. Dad complaining about the tire salesman at the car dealership. A rant about the Russians and communism.

Dad must've kept this in secret. He guessed Mom was the only person who knew about it. The guys at work would've crucified him if they knew Dad kept a journal. That just wasn't something men did in his father's day. He decided to read a bit more. The scratchy handwriting was tough on Jesse's eyes, but he kept going.

Woke up to take care of business in the middle of the night. Far enough from the tent not to attract animals. As I was standing there watering the tree, I heard the most God-awful howl. I mean, it gave me shivers. I finished up my business and hurried back to the tent. Thinking maybe it was some sort of animal mating or in heat. Or in terrible pain. Whatever it was, I didn't want to be around if it came calling.

Thinking of moving camp in the morning. Gonna try and get some sleep. Maybe coming here alone wasn't a good idea. Time will tell.

Jesse gave his father credit for not packing up and heading out right there. Of course, he couldn't have known what lurked in the woods. It could've been a mountain lion or an elk. Not that a mountain lion lurking around was desirable, but at least there was some familiarity with it. He decided that little bit was enough for tonight. Made a mental note to set up an appointment with Dr. Lowe at the eye clinic. Maybe he'd see what was on the tube. Try and take his mind off things.

Gina waited her turn to shoot. They'd decided to play pool, men versus women. David was currently lining up the nine ball. Steve stood next to Gina, a beer bottle in hand. Priya stood behind David as he lined up his shot.

"Looking fine, Doctor," Priya said.

"You're distracting me."

She gave him a playful nudge with her hip. "How about now?"

"I believe this constitutes cheating," David said.

"Definitely not in the rules," Steve said. "The ladies should be disqualified."

They'd put on some music. A nineties playlist. Kurt Cobain was currently wailing in the background. Gina missed the grunge era. It had all seemed so fresh and exciting when that Seattle music broke. Dangerous. Stuff that would piss off your parents. Now you could buy a Nirvana t-shirt in Target. She often wondered if the teens she saw wearing band tees had ever listened to said bands.

David sank the nine ball. He circled the table, planning his next shot.

"I'm gonna grab a beer," Gina said. "You're doing a great job of getting things in the hole, David."

David's face flushed. Priya burst out laughing.

"Stop trying to fluster my partner," Steve said.

Gina headed to the fridge, opened it, and grabbed a bottle of beer. She popped the top with an opener and took a swig. Over at the pool table, David missed his next shot, which drew applause from Priya.

Something thudded against the house, and Gina flinched.

"What the hell?" Steve said.

A second thump sounded against the cabin's rear wall. Gina retreated from the kitchen and joined the others near the pool table. The thump was followed a moment later by a deep roar. Gina set her beer on a table and ran upstairs for one of the guns. She came back down with the semiautomatic.

Another whack shook the cabin's side.

"Turn the lights off," Priya said.

David and Steve went around and hit the lights, plunging the cabin into darkness.

"Is it trying to break in?" David said.

"Don't know," Gina said.

Gina eyed the French doors leading onto the deck. They were all glass. Wouldn't be hard for a large animal to break in. Maybe they should've left. Their moment of fun and relaxation over a game of pool was shattered. Another thud came, this time high on the outside wall. That had to be the second story. She realized something was throwing objects against the cabin.

Steve went to the front windows. He peered outside.

"See anything?" David asked.

"Nothing out front."

"I'm going to have a look from upstairs," Gina said, and headed up. She went to the bathroom window, which would provide a good view of the rear of the property. She got glimpses of the woods through the blowing snow. No sign of the intruder.

She heard someone come upstairs. A moment later, Steve joined her in the bathroom, holding the shotgun.

"Anything?" he said.

"Can't see much."

"Thinking we should get the cops out here."

"Not a bad idea this time."

They headed downstairs, where Priya was already on the phone with nine-one-one. Way ahead of them. Priya finished the call and said,

"They're sending out a patrol car. Needless to say, they told us not to go outside."

"Damn, I was thinking we could take a hike," David said.

Priya shot him a stern look.

"Did you spot anything?" Priya said.

"Couldn't see much with the snow," Gina said.

Another object struck the cabin. It sounded like a small car hitting the exterior. "Jesus," Gina said.

"What the hell is it throwing?" Steve said.

David said, "No idea, but we're out of here in the morning."

They waited a few minutes. No more thuds came. A knock came at the cabin's door. She set the gun down, then answered and found two police officers on the porch. In the driveway, two patrol SUVs were parked behind David and Priya's Jeep.

"You heard noises outside?" the lead cop said. He was tall with spiky hair.

"Something keeps slamming against the wall. Sounds like something's being thrown," Gina said.

The officer behind the spiky-haired cop had a sleek-looking, black shotgun.

"Which direction were they coming from?" the spiky-haired cop said.

Gina pointed to the wall. "At the rear, too."

"We'll have a look around," the lead cop said.

Gina shut the door. The four of them gathered around a side window, which would give them a view of the police. She watched them trudge through the snow, shining flashlights into the woods. They moved toward the trees, disappearing into the snow.

"I don't envy them," David said.

A few moments passed before a shotgun boomed outside. The four of them gasped in unison.

"Jesus," Gina said.

She heard yelling, caught up in the wind. Then metal and glass being smashed out in the driveway. Sounded like someone dropped a dumpster off a roof. What the hell was that? Two more gunshots echoed from outside. More yelling. Another shot. She heard footsteps out front and raced to the windows. The police ran back to their vehicles. The spiky-haired cop was leaning inside his patrol SUV.

To her surprise, a boulder rested on top of the Jeep's roof, which had crumpled like a crushed beer can. Smashed glass glinted in the moonlight.

The cop headed back to the cabin's front door. Gina opened it. "What's going on?"

"We spotted something, but it took off. Afraid it looped around and ruined that Jeep out there."

"David, Priya, you'll want to see this."

Priya arrived at the door and gasped at the sight of the ruined Jeep. David joined them, and upon seeing the Jeep, said, "Holy shit, it's totaled! Our Jeep!"

"We're requesting backup. Stay inside."

"What exactly did you find?" Gina said.

"We chased a large animal on two legs. It disappeared into the snow," the officer said. "Stay put and lock the doors in case it comes back."

That wouldn't do much good. If that thing could throw a boulder, smashing through doors wouldn't be a problem.

"What the hell are we going to do now?" David said.

"Sucks about the car, man," Steve said.

"We have a bigger problem," Priya said. "Whatever's out in the woods is big and angry."

"We're not going anywhere tonight," Gina said. "And the police are working on it."

"That's something, I suppose," David said. "How the hell am I going to explain this to my insurance?"

Rodgers got the call in the middle of the night. Their mystery creature was at it again. Seems it was harassing the people at the big log home out on Route 78. He'd gotten up and dressed, poked his head in and told the girls he was going on a call, and headed to the patrol SUV.

He made his way to the log home, fighting the blowing snow every step of the way. After a ten-minute drive, he pulled up behind several Barker police vehicles. One of his guys briefed him. They'd pursued the thing into the woods, where it looped back and tossed a large rock on a parked car. After that, they'd pursued it again, opening fire. It had then disappeared into the snow.

On the drive over, he'd gotten the okay from the chief to organize a party and go after the intruder. He had five officers on the scene, besides himself. He saw the evidence of the creature's fury in the form of a boulder that had crushed a green Jeep.

He instructed his people to take their shotguns. Wasn't sure if that was adequate or not. They couldn't let the thing roam the woods and keep threatening people. It had already killed one person.

Schwartz, with his spiky hair, came over with his shotgun. He jammed a winter cap on, thereby ruining his hairstyle.

"Where's the last place you saw it?" Rodgers said.

"We followed it up a ridge off that way, about a hundred yards. Then we lost it."

"I don't want to go too deep in, between the snow and the darkness. Plus, we only have six guys here. I'd like more."

"I don't think we hit it," Schwartz said.

"I want to have a look at the cabin wall."

Schwartz followed Rodgers to the side of the cabin. A number of good-sized rocks lay in the snow, some of them comparable to landscape boulders. Gouges raked the log wall. "Damn. Why throw the rocks?"

"Intimidation?" Schwartz said.

"Could be. I think if these people were smart, they'd vacate. Not going anywhere with that Jeep."

"Not to question you, Lieutenant, but shouldn't we get more guys if we're going in there."

"I want to have a look," Rodgers said. "These people are in danger."

Rodgers headed back to the patrol vehicles and the men gathered around him. "Keep it tight out there. We can't see much. And keep talking. You spot anything, call it out, got it?"

The men nodded. Rodgers led the way, heading into the woods. It was slow going with the snow, and it wasn't long before his legs were on fire from exertion. The tip of his nose and cheeks felt numb.

Have to start a leg day at the gym. And a ski mask wouldn't hurt.

"Are we on the right track?" Rodgers asked Schwartz.

"This is the direction, yeah."

The wind lashed his face. This was frostbite weather. They started up a ridge. That's when he got a whiff of it. Like sewer mixed with barn animals. "Hold up. Just got a whiff."

He scanned the woods. Couldn't see too much through the curtain of snow. Maybe they should come back at first light with more guys, or request a helicopter from the state.

A grunt came from his left. Then a gurgling scream. He turned and saw Greg Andres, one of his senior officers, lying in the snow. Blood gushed from a gash in his head. A large rock lay in the snow next to Andres. Schwartz knelt by Andres. Another rock flew from the trees. Rodgers ducked, and it sailed over his head.

He fired a blast in the direction the rock had come from.

A huge roar bellowed from the trees.

Andres was muttering something. Not making much sense. He'd taken a solid blow to the dome. A third rock sailed toward them and struck Pete Coulier in the thigh. Coulier grunted and stumbled backward, landing on his ass in the snow. He bounced back up, limping.

"You hurt, Pete?" Rodgers said, scanning the woods for any sign of the creature.

"I'm okay. Nothing broke. Gonna have a hell of a bruise."

"We need to get Andres out of here," Rodgers said.

"He's got a head injury. Should we move him?"

"Yeah we should fucking move him," Rodgers said. "EMTs ain't coming in here with that thing running around. Get him up."

A bigger rock flew at them, striking a tree and chipping off bark. The wind brought with it the stink of the monster. They wouldn't be bottling that scent for cologne any time soon. Rodgers almost gagged.

Schwartz and one of his other guys got Andres to his feet. His head slumped forward. Rodgers radioed and requested an ambulance at the log home's address. Told them officer down.

They retreated. Rodgers fired blindly into the woods. No more rocks came flying, but the creature let out a howl that pierced Rodgers' core. That was goddamned terrifying.

Rodgers and his men made it back to the driveway. Andres was moaning, and they set him in the passenger seat of a patrol vehicle to get him out of the cold. A moment later, he heard the ambulance's siren wailing and it pulled in and parked behind the line of police vehicles. Two EMTs hopped out carrying bags with their gear.

"Over here!" Rodgers said, waving them to the police SUV. They went to work examining Andres, getting pressure on his wound to stop the bleeding.

A young EMT said, "What happened to him?"

"Something threw a rock at him."

"Something? You mean someone?"

"You heard me right the first time," Rodgers said. He stood behind the EMTs and let them work. "How you doing, Andres?"

"I'm gonna live, I think," he mumbled. "Did the lift take us down?"

He's talking about skiing. "No, we walked."

The second EMT, a woman with short, bleached hair, kept pressure on Andres' wound. The young EMT said, "Lieutenant, mind helping me grab the gurney so my partner can work on him?"

"You got it."

They went to the ambulance and grabbed the gurney, carrying it, wheels folded up. No way were they getting it through the snow. The EMTs got Andres loaded on it, and along with the EMTs, Rodgers and Schwartz helped carry him to the ambulance.

"I'll follow them," Schwartz said.

"Keep me posted. Call his wife, will you?"

"I'll let her know what's going on."

The ambulance pulled out. The driveway was wide enough to allow Schwartz to sneak his vehicle out. He watched the ambulance pull out, lights flashing. The siren kicked in. Schwartz followed the ambulance.

Hopefully Andres would be okay. Lynn would be a nervous wreck. She and Andres had been married something like thirty-five years. She still packed Andres a lunch in a cooler every day. Sometimes she put little notes in there, a source of amusement for the entire force. *Love you. Be safe.* Andres took quite a bit of good-natured crap for the love notes, although Rodgers suspected some of the guys were a little envious. Many of them were single guys who either hit the bars or went home to empty apartments post-shift.

Rodgers glanced at the log home. The occupants were standing at the front window, peering out, looking hopeful. Wished he had good news for them. He went to the door, and when they saw him coming, the dark-haired, petite woman opened it.

Twelve

"I saw the ambulance," Gina said to Rodgers.

"We had an officer down."

"Did you find anything?"

Rodgers' skin looked pale. He stuck his hands in his pockets, presumably to stop them from shaking. He let out a big sigh.

"It threw rocks at us. Clipped one of my guys in the head."

"Will he be okay?"

"Hopefully. I'm afraid your Jeep is totaled."

David brushed passed her and Rodgers. He'd put his boots on at some point. "I'm going to have a look."

"Sir, I recommend staying inside."

David was already on his way to the Jeep. "Son of a bitch," he said. "Only made six payments on her."

"I don't recommend staying here," Rodgers said. "I can keep an officer parked here for a bit, but I'm going to need him back pretty soon."

"We'll discuss it," Gina said.

It would be dangerous to stay here, but they were without a ride. She supposed she could call her sister in Buffalo, but she was two hours away. "Is there a taxi service out here. Ride sharing?"

"No taxi, but you could try Uber. There's a hotel in town. Nothing fancy, but it's clean and reasonable," Rodgers said.

Priya joined David at the Jeep. Mostly they stared in silence, as if mourning the loss of the jeep. The air freshener that had hung from the mirror now lay on the hood. Snowflakes clung to the boulder, and it Reminded Gina of a snowman's bottom half.

"Why don't you folks head inside?" Rodgers said.

Priya and David filtered back into the lodge, David with his arm around her.

"Will you be here much longer?" Gina asked.

"For a bit. Like I said, I'll leave an officer behind to keep an eye out."

Gina thanked him and Rodgers went back to his business. They gathered in the kitchen. The rock throwing incident had shaken her. Probably not much chance of getting a ride share this time of night in a storm, so they'd likely be staying the night. "Do we stay or go?"

"I have to at least wait around until they can haul the car out of here," David said.

"He's right. They're going to have to put it on a flatbed," Priya said.

"We'll stay with you guys. Not leaving," Steve said.

"Hadn't thought of the car getting hauled," Gina said. "We'll definitely hang with you."

"You'd better," Priya said with a wry smile. "You've got the damned guns."

"Do you think it wants to get in here?" David said.

"I think if it wanted in, it would do it. Maybe it's being territorial, trying to scare us off," Gina said.

"Maybe I'll stand watch," Steve said.

"Bigfoot duty. Jesus, who would've thought?" David said.

"Anyone up for some more beers?" Priya said.

They all agreed to that.

Madison Cowers hated the shitty little mobile home they lived in, but at least she had it to herself tonight. Mom was working second shift at Presto Electric, where she worked on the line making switches. It was the weekend, and she was going to watch all the horror movies her mom disapproved of. Stay up all night. Tonight it would be *Dog Soldiers* followed by *Dawn of the Dead*.

She peeked out her bedroom window, which faced the woods behind the mobile home. Still snowing like hell out there. She went into the kitchen, looked out that window. The rest of the trailer park was dark, except for a light from the Stanton's trailer across the way.

She hated the trailer park. Mainly hated what the other kids said to her about living here. It hadn't been so bad in elementary school. She'd had a tight knit group of friends, but they'd gone their separate ways freshman year of high school. Once some of the kids at the high school found out where she lived, Madison got officially dubbed trailer trash. Or mobile home queen.

Not like any of them were rich. They just didn't live in a fucking mobile home like she did. Therefore, she was the lowest of the low.

Oh well, fuck them for now. She had the place to herself. In the kitchen, she threw a bag of popcorn in the microwave. While the popcorn was popping, she grabbed a Mountain Dew from the fridge. Her snacks in hand, she sat in front of the television and queued up *Dog Soldiers*.

The movie began to play. She ate a few handfuls of popcorn. From outside came a thump. It made her jump, and she spilled some popcorn on the couch.

"Shit," she said, and picked up the popcorn, placing it back in the bowl.

The thump was followed by a low growl.

"What the hell?"

She paused the movie and looked out the side window. Nothing out there except snow. She stood there and listened for a few moments. No more growling. Maybe she'd been hearing things with the wind gusting.

She sat on the couch and played the movie. It was almost to the opening scene when she became aware of someone at the window. She turned and saw a massive, hairy face peering in at her. Large, red eyes. Madison screamed and dropped the popcorn bowl, scattering pieces all over the rug.

The face dissolved into the snow. She fished her phone from her pocket. Dropped it on the table. Picked it up and dialed nine-one-one.

Another growl came from outside.

"What's your emergency?" the dispatcher said.

"There's someone outside my trailer. They were looking in the window at me."

"Are they still there?"

"I think so. I'm home alone. Please hurry."

"Did you lock your doors?"

"I'll lock it now," Madison said.

She locked the trailer's side door. Right after she locked it, the trailer began to shake. It was like a damned earthquake. A few glasses fell from the drainboard and smashed on the floor. Mom's potted fern on and end table dumped, spilling soil on the rug. Felt like a damned earthquake.

"Someone's shaking the whole trailer!"

"An officer is on the way. Is anyone else home?"

"Just me."

The shaking stopped. Madison's heart felt like it might burst from beating so hard. Tears streamed down her face. She backed away from the door and waited.

"I'll stay on the phone until the officer arrives," the dispatcher said. "What's happening now?"

"It stopped. Quiet."

The wind screamed outside. Something like small rocks pelted the trailer. Probably ice from the storm. She took some deep breaths, trying to calm herself. The police would be here soon.

She pressed herself against the wall, right next to the bookshelf where Mom kept her romance novels. Another roar shook the trailer and a dark, hairy fist smashed through the window next to her. She darted across the room. The hand reached blindly for her. A rotten smell wafted into the trailer.

Madison ran to her bedroom at the rear of the mobile home. She slammed the door. Would it try and get inside? She slipped into the closet and shut the door. The trailer shook a few more times. After a while, she heard radios squawking and men's voices outside.

The police were here.

She waited a few moments in the closet, then someone banged on the door and said, "Barker Police!"

Madison slipped out of the closet and answered the door. A young officer with strawberry blonde hair stood at the door, his gun drawn.

"Is it out there?" Madison said.

"The intruder?"

"The thing, the monster."

"Stay inside. We're going to have a look."

The officer disappeared along the side of the trailer. While she had a moment, she called the plant. The night security guard answered. Madison told her it was an emergency and she needed to talk to her mother.

"Hang on," the guy said in a bored voice, and put her on hold. She waited a bit, and then her mom answered.

"What's going on? Are you hurt? They got me off the line."

"Something tried to get in the trailer. An animal. The police are here."

"Are - are you ok?"

"I'm not hurt, just scared," Madison said. "Can you come home?"

"I'll be there as soon as I can. I'll tell Carl what's going on."

Carl was a mega-asshole who gave the employees a hard time over everything. Call-ins, wanting time off, being a minute late for work. Hopefully he'd let mom leave.

"Hurry up."

"I'll do my best."

They ended the call. The police officer returned, stepping inside the trailer. He had snow crusted on his pants up to the knees. He had a flashlight in one hand and his gun in another.

"I followed tracks to the wood's edge. Wasn't going after it by myself."

"Did you see it?"

"No, just the tracks. I see it smashed the window."

"It shook the whole trailer, too. I was sitting down to watch a movie when I heard it. Then it was staring at me."

"Are your parents home?"

"My mom's on her way from work. My dad lives out of state."

"I'll wait around for your mom to get here."

"What if it comes back?" Madison said.

"Call us. There's been a few other similar incidents in town."

She didn't want to stay here, but they didn't have anywhere else to go. When Mom pulled up fifteen minutes later, she breathed a sigh of relief. Mom hurried into the trailer and embraced Madison. They didn't hug much these days, but she let Mom embrace her. She began to cry again.

"It's okay. We'll figure this out," Mom said.

Monique had been taking notes as the police scanner chattered. Earlier, there'd been a report of someone throwing rocks at a house. Police had responded. Then, a few moments ago, the report of an intruder and a broken window at a mobile home. She'd scribbled the addresses, hoping to later speak with the people involved.

James came back in. He'd gone down the road to grab some burgers and fries for them at McDonald's. His coat was dusted with snow. He held two paper bags and a tray with Cokes in it. The food smelled amazing, even if it was just Mickey D's. Her stomach growled.

"Got you a Quarter Pounder," James said. "Dropped Kurt's off at his room."

"Appreciate it. Our friend has been at it again. Report of an intruder at a mobile home park."

"Damn, he's busy."

"Or she. We don't know."

"When's the boss getting here?"

"Probably sometime tomorrow afternoon."

"Think he'll swoop in and take credit?"

"Likely."

"My father called me while I was out," James said.

"Doesn't he sleep? What'd he say?"

"He stays up half the night reading scripture and writing sermons. Got the same. Wasting my life. Not paying attention to my calling. I got off the phone quick."

"Still wants you to follow the Lord."

"Well I asked the Lord, and he wants me out here. We're part of a major scientific discovery, and you caught it on tape."

Monique dug through the bag and pulled out her burger. The paper was grease-stained and the burger smelled delicious. She unwrapped it and took a bite. James joined her at the table and took his burger from the bag.

"You excited?" James said, through a mouthful of cheeseburger.

"Hell yeah I'm excited. This is for real."

"What if we take a ride out to that crime scene?"

"I'm sure the cops would love that," James said.

"Just a quick look. If it's being watched, we'll turn around."

"All right," James said. "We should maybe talk to the people at the trailer, too."

"If the boss lets us."

"Man, fuck him. We're doing the leg work here."

"You gonna tell him that?" Monique said.

"Naw, I like my job."

"The job we don't get paid for," she said.

"Bigfoot researcher sounds cool, though."

Maybe they'd get their own television show out of this. They ate the burgers and fries. When they were done, they turned on the flatscreen and sat on the bed, both leaning against pillows propped against the headboard.

Monique flipped through the channels. Nothing really on. Then they came to a local channel with a breaking news item. A pretty, blonde reporter stood at the edge of a driveway, snow whipping around her. They were on the scene where police had responded to someone throwing rocks at a log home.

Police had chased the intruder into the woods and fired shots. Backup officers also responded. After heading into the woods, one of them was taken to the hospital after being struck by a large rock. The intruder fled.

"Damn," James said. "Did you pick that up on the scanner?"

"Not the part about the police chasing it into the woods."

"It's heating up."

"For sure. I'm excited. You?"

"Yeah, not looking forward to going off in the damned woods, though."

"This one's aggressive," Monique said.

"I'm not about to die out there."

"We're not gonna die. Wanna see what's on demand? Rent a movie?"

"Sure, just no Bigfoot flicks."

Thirteen

Roland rolled out of his cot and headed to the showers. After showering and brushing his teeth, he grabbed a cup of coffee and took a seat in the makeshift cafeteria. He was looking forward to seeing Alex. Getting back to life and not living in a tent. The minutes couldn't go by fast enough.

He spotted Gus Carrigan, one of the long-time volunteers at the center. Gus nodded hello and headed to the table. He took a seat, grunting as he plopped down.

"Damned knees aren't what they used to be," Gus said.

Gus was somewhere north of seventy. He pasted the remaining hair on his head down with some sort of greasy product. A pair of copper bands graced his wrist.

"Age catches up with all of us," Roland said.

"Hear about the excitement in town?"

"How's that?"

"People got their door bashed in. Some girl got attacked at her trailer."

Roland knew where this was going. He wasn't going to mention his experience with the creature. "Who do they think did it?"

"Not who, what. That bugger that lives in the woods."

"You're a believer."

"I believe my eyes.

"You've seen it?"

Gus nodded solemnly.

"Wanna tell me about it?"

"I guess it wasn't much, really. I was driving back from Cleveland with Janey. This was fifteen, sixteen years ago. We'd hit the outskirts of town, out on route seventy-eight. It was a bit foggy, around nine-thirty at night. Well, I come around a bend and something walks across the road. I hit the brakes. It was huge. Lots of hair. Turned its head, looked at us, and was gone in a few strides. I sat there, shocked as shit for a minute, until Janey shook my arm and told me to get going. In case it came back," Gus said, and swigged his coffee.

Based on the encounter Roland had, Gus had been lucky. "Never saw it again?"

"Nope, but my brother had a scarier encounter."

"What happened?"

"He was a lineman, you know, working electrical towers. Him and his partner had to climb a tower just north of town. By the time they got done, it was getting dark. Well, they stash their gear and hop in the truck. By now, it's dark and Hank just wants to get home to dinner. He hears something growl behind the truck, looks in the side mirror, and sees it standing there."

"What did he do?"

"He beat it the hell out of there. It chased them down the service road for a bit. Hank thought it was just trying to scare them off, said it could've caught up if it wanted to. He refused to service that tower after that. Eventually got a job selling cars at the Ford dealership in Barker."

The more stories Roland heard, the more he was glad to be leaving. Especially after his own encounter. "Did I tell you I'm leaving?"

"Leaving the shelter?"

"Leaving town. My brother's picking me up. Has a job waiting for me."

"That's great news, Roland. Happy for you. You want another coffee? I'm buying."

The coffee – like everything else – was free at the shelter. Gus never tired of the "I'm buying" joke, though.

"I'll take another."

Gus took Roland's empty cup and headed to the kitchen window to get more coffee. He returned with two Styrofoam cups, steam rising from both.

"Almost forgot, someone got killed up in that Applewood subdivision."

"What happened?"

"News didn't say. Just they found a body and they were going to have to use DNA to get a positive ID. Guess they were in bad shape. Guy got killed going to pick up some tools."

"I'm glad to be leaving, honestly."

"You ever see anything funny in your travels? You spent a lot of time outdoors."

"Can't say I have," Roland said, sipping the steaming coffee.

He felt bad for lying to Gus, but he didn't really want to talk about it. He was looking forward to his fresh start with Alex and the new job. Ready to put the town of Barker and his life on the streets behind him.

Jesse and Tim decided to meet Teri out at his place so she could have a look at the door. Tim took a half day from work. Brian stayed back, as he had a project to finish for his job. They stopped for lunch at Izzy's, a little place that served manhole-sized pancakes with real maple syrup. They also had burgers so large a Python would have trouble getting its jaws around them. Jesse kept it light, eating half a club and some minestrone.

Isabel Duncan, the owner, kept a cardboard bigfoot cutout near the checkout counter as a joke. Ordinarily, Jesse thought the thing to be silly, a cartoonish horror creature. The experience the other day had changed his mind. He was glad to be back on the road and not have the thing staring at him, however goofy the cutout seemed.

When they pulled up to the house, Teri's red Dodge Ram was parked in the driveway. She hopped out, dressed in a tan Carhartt coat, jeans, and work boots. Her dark hair spilled out from under a winter cap. She shook both their hands.

"How's business?" Tim asked.

"A little slow. Finished up a bathroom remodel yesterday. Not much else on the slate right now."

"I'm glad you could get to the door," Jesse said.

"Tim said you had some excitement."

"A little more than I wanted."

"That damned thing is apparently running all around town," Teri said.

"What do you think of this?"

"Got a shotgun mounted on a rack in the truck, if that tells you. Let's have a peek at your door."

Teri grabbed a toolbox from the truck and they headed around back. Using a screw gun, she removed the tarp and plywood. Tim gave her a hand setting the sheet of plywood aside.

She measured the frame, jotting down the numbers on a small pad she took from her pocket. "This is standard. Depot should have something in stock. I can put this in for you tomorrow morning if all goes well."

"I want something solid. No glass."

"Like a garage entry door?" Teri said.

"Something like that. How much are we talking?"

"You get right down to business," Teri said with a laugh. "I like that."

"I'll get you a price on the door. Labor is sixty an hour. My partner's gonna help. I'll text you tonight with the full price. Sound good? Won't beat you up too bad."

"Appreciate this," Jesse said.

"My pleasure."

"You gonna be okay out here?" Jesse asked. "With that thing running around?"

"I won't be alone. Got the twelve gauge in the truck, plus Sam will be with me. Us ladies can handle ourselves, believe it or not."

"I wasn't doubting you," Jesse said.

"You'd be surprised how many guys see a woman contractor and feel the need to 'help out' with things. One jackass called me honey one time and asked if I was okay using the circular saw."

Tim said, "Did you saw him in half?"

Teri laughed, "I told him honey was for damned bears and he'd best stay the hell out of my way."

"I like your style, Teri," Jesse said.

"We'll get you fixed up and back home in no time."

They pulled up to the house on Applewood Lane. Police tape had been crossed over the door. Monique didn't see any police around, but that didn't mean they wouldn't be patrolling. Other than the tape across the door, it was appeared to be an average suburban home. Beige siding with maroon shudders. Flowers hand-painted on the mailbox. Most of the homes in the subdivision were of similar styling.

"Why are we here again?" Kurt said.

"Documentation," Monique said.

"Gonna get us arrested," Kurt grumbled.

"We'll be fine," Monique said.

"Kinda with Kurt on this one," James said. "Cops won't like us poking around a crime scene."

"I won't go in. Just want to check out the property."

Kurt let out an aggravated sigh. "I think we should wait for the boss man to get here before we do anything else."

"Just a quick look," Monique said.

"You don't often talk her out of things, do you?" Kurt said.

"Once she's made up her mind, forget it."

Monique slipped out of the vehicle, digital video cam in hand. She planned to narrate as she checked out the house. Might not find anything, but she didn't want to miss documenting it. Never know what you'd find.

She crossed the street under the steady snowfall. It provided her some cover. None of the neighbors were outside. In the distance, the put-put of a snowblower engine filled the air. She heard James say something, but it was muffled in the wind.

No one watching, which suited her fine. She crossed the front yard and rounded the house. There was a patio in back, and some plywood had been tacked up over the doors. That must've been where it entered.

Monique pressed her face against a kitchen window. She could see through to the living room, where a dark stain had blotted the rug. She shivered. That's where the guy had met his end.

She'd never read of a legitimate documented attack inside a home. The famous Fouke monster supposedly attacked a family member outside the home. The victim had been taken to the hospital in shock, unable to speak. She wasn't aware of a Sasquatch breaking into a home. Of course, it was getting harder to filter out legitimate stories. It seemed like hundreds of people had podcasts or YouTube channels filled with tales of monster sightings.

She filmed through the window, trying to capture the blood stain on camera. "Looking through the rear kitchen window at a bloodstain on the carpet."

Not sure how good that would show up on video.

She stepped to the patio doors. The wind rattled the plywood. Also got the door on video, saying, "This is where it's believed the Sasquatch entered the house."

Monique examined the doorframe, looking for any sign of hair or blood. The more evidence, the better. She was aware of a rotten odor in the air. Smelled like an animal. Maybe it was time to get out of here. It could've been lingering odor, or the thing could be around, maybe watching her now.

As she turned, she saw it charge from the woods at the yard's edge. She started to bolt, but it was on her in seconds. The creature swung a massive fist and swatted her to the ground. The snow cushioned her fall. The camera tumbled and landed lens-down in the snow.

Her head swam with dizziness. It picked her up and she was aware of being carried away from the house. She tried to scream, but it slapped a hand over her mouth. The leathery skin had an earthy stink to it.

Monique struggled, but the beast clamped down, squeezing her until it her chest felt like it might burst. She tried to breathe, but her chest was compressed. After a few moments of running through the woods, it relaxed its grip and she breathed easier.

Still had no idea where it was taking her. She was in trouble. That much was true. Through the trees, the house diminished in size, and with each step, she was that much farther from safety.

The beast carried her for some time, going uphill and grunting the whole time. Her face was pressed into its matted fur, and the stench made her eyes water. They went deep into the woods, and eventually it stopped and set her down. It towered over her. Shoved her backward, and she landed on her ass in the snow.

It roared, indicating its displeasure. She turned and saw a structure made of sticks and leaves. Dome-shaped with a small opening.

The creature came closer. She scrambled on hands and knees. It crouched and roared at her again, which shook her whole frame. After a moment, she realized it wanted her to crawl inside the dome, and she did so. The floor inside was dirt with some scattered pine needles. A strong, animal-like stink filled the shelter.

It peered in at her, bearing its pointed incisors that looked capable of crushing rocks. After a moment, it loped off into the woods. She squeezed herself against the wall, as far away from the opening as possible. She shivered. Luckily she had her heavy coat, gloves, and a hat. Even so, it was freezing in here.

After some time passed, she dared crawling to the opening. Worth having a look to try and gauge her location. A peek out the doorway showed nothing but snow and dense woods. She might as well be on the surface of Mars. The snow was two-to-three feet deep in all directions. Walking out of here – even if she could remain undetected – would be exhausting.

She slipped back into the shelter and dug her phone from her pocket. Tried to dial James' number but got no signal. She wouldn't even know where to tell him to look for her.

Monique slipped the phone back her pocket. She leaned against the wall and drew her knees in, hugging herself and trying to conserve warmth.

What did it want with her? Why drag her off to the woods? Some of the possibilities made her shudder. She would rather collapse and freeze to death in the snow than face whatever horrible things the creature had in store. She wasn't dying in some stinking hut woven from sticks and leaves.

She'd gouge its eyes out if it came to that. At least go down fighting.

Kurt leaned forward. "You gonna go check on her or am I?"

"How about we both go?"

Kurt figured Monique was probably fine, just caught up in investigating the house, but the longer they lingered, the greater the chance of being spotted. They didn't need the cops up their asses.

Working with the research foundation had been a nice little diversion for Kurt. He'd retired after twenty years in the Marine Corps, then drove dump trucks before calling it a career. Working with the Organization got him outdoors, and it had its moments. Besides, these young kids needed someone like him. Most of them didn't know a firearm from a hole in their ass. You didn't go wandering around the woods with no protection.

Even if they'd never seen a Bigfoot, there were still nasty things in parts of the country. Bears. Wolves. Mountain lions. He was glad to teach them. Monique and James were good kids. Fast learners. But she had been stubborn, and they'd overstayed their welcome here.

He and James got out and crossed the street. Kurt raised the collar of his jacket against the wind. Could use a good nip of bourbon right about now. They headed to the back yard, slogging through the snow.

No sign of Monique in the back yard or on the patio. Plywood covered the broken patio glass door.

"Monique?" James said.

"Hope she wasn't fool enough to go in the house."

"She's no fool."

James examined the patio. "Oh, shit."

"What?" Kurt said.

"Look at this."

Monique's video camera lay in the snow. Even more concerning were the nearly twenty-inch footprints nearby. They led away from the house and into the woods.

They circled the perimeter of the house, even peering in the windows, and found no sign of Monique. Dread settled in Kurt's gut as he realized she'd been taken. "We need to grab the guns and go after her."

"Then let's go," James said.

Back at the truck, Kurt strapped on a .44 revolver and grabbed a shotgun from the rack. James grabbed a 9mm semiautomatic that was in a shoulder rig. He put it on under his jacket.

"Goddamn, I should've gone with her."

"We both should've. Couldn't have known that would happen," Kurt said. "Important thing is that we find her."

They locked up the truck and hurried back behind the house, following the tracks to the woods' edge. Kurt spotted where the branches and brush had been trampled, and the footprints continued. It could've taken her anywhere. With luck, she was still alive.

"Follow me," Kurt said.

They followed the tracks, slogging through the deep snow. Within moments, Kurt was breathing hard. Same with James. They stopped, rested with hands on knees, bent over. This was going to be a bitch. After resting, they followed the tracks for another hundred yards or so.

Kurt's heart was working overtime. Not a young man anymore. Even with the cold weather, sweat trickled down his back.

"C'mon," James said.

"Wait," Kurt said. "We have no supplies. It's storming still. And we can't move through the snow with any speed."

"So we just leave her?"

"No, but we should report it."

"And tell the cops we were at a crime scene?"

"We didn't actually go in. Probably get a slap on the hand," Kurt said.

James looked at the trail ahead. Seemed to be pondering things. A large predator like the Sasquatch could move rapidly and unimpeded through the snow. Not so much for Kurt and James. His knees ached and his legs burned. He was doing his best to catch his breath.

"Ok. We call."

They retreated to the yard and Kurt dialed nine-one-one. He gave the dispatcher the information, feeling like an idiot reporting abduction by Sasquatch. They said they'd be sending an officer right away.

Roland had his backpack with his few possessions slung over his shoulder. He waited in the vestibule at the Hope Center. Alex pulled up in his Blue Yukon. He climbed out and shuffled across the icy sidewalk, dressed in a black parka with a furry hood. His jeans were tucked into knee-high Muck boots.

Alex wrenched the door from the wind. His brother had gotten gray since Roland last saw him. A whisp of a comb-over covered his balding dome.

"Hey, brother," Roland said.

"Jesus Christ if it isn't the wanderer himself!" Alex said. He grabbed Roland in a bear hug. Roland did his best to return the hug. He realized it had been years since he'd hugged anyone, romantic or not.

Alex released the hug. Roland felt it in his ribs.

"So, you need to check out or anything?"

"It's not a hotel. I can leave whenever."

"That all your stuff?"

"Everything in the world."

"We'll go shopping. I'll loan you some money for clothes and all that."

"I appreciate it."

"They're excited to meet you at the plant. Got your interview scheduled for next week, from what they tell me. Don't worry, the job's yours. Interview is just a formality."

That filled him with dread. The thought of a job interview made his hands clammy thinking about it. Another thing he hadn't done in an age. "Here's hoping I don't blow it."

"You'll be great. Ready? Gonna take a bit in this weather."

Outside, Roland loaded his pack in the back seat. They hopped in the Yukon and Alex started it up. The truck had only been sitting a few minutes, but already snow crusted the windshield. Alex turned on the wipers and they sliced through the snow.

Alex drove out of town, heading out Route 78. The business district gave way to scattered homes, and soon dense forest lined both sides of the road. He kept the Yukon at a steady forty miles per hour.

"Snow is something, isn't it?" Alex said.

"Glad I'm not out in it."

The snow intensified over the next few minutes. Alex dropped his speed down to twenty. He turned up the wipers. It was as if someone had dropped a white blanket in front of the windshield. Alex leaned forward and squinted, as if it would increase his visual acuity in the snow.

"Damn. I'm thinking we should get off the road," Alex said.

"We just got started."

"You see how bad it is?"

"Guess I can't argue that," Roland said. "There's a hotel about a mile up."

The Bear's Den Motor Lodge. Roland had stayed there one night years ago. He'd bought a scratch off ticket on a whim and won two hundred bucks. With his winnings, he'd stayed a few nights at the motor lodge.

"I'm thinking we might be better off waiting it out."

"I stayed there once. It's decent."

Alex drove them another mile and Roland guided them to the lodge. They managed to spot the driveway through the blowing snow and Alex eased the Yukon into the lot. The sign indicated they had vacancy. A Volkswagen Jetta was the only other car parked in the lot.

Alex parked near the motel office. They headed inside, hurrying to get out of the wind. A woman with blonde, curly hair sat behind the desk. She was about forty. Wore a flannel shirt with the sleeves rolled up. Several bracelets graced each wrist.

"Help you gentlemen?"

"Need a room. The storm was a little too much."

"One room?"

"That'll do," Alex said.

"Surprised you don't have more guests," Roland said. "Weary travelers in a storm."

"Business has been rough lately. People don't like hearing noises at night."

"What do you mean?" Roland asked.

"Something's been creeping around at night. Couple people had something banging on their doors outside. Called the cops multiple times, but it's always gone by the time they get here."

"Well, we're not scared of a few noises. We'll take that room," Alex said.

In truth, Roland wished they hadn't gotten caught in the storm. After the incident with the creature outside his tent, he wanted to be away from the Barker area.

The clerk checked them in and Alex put the room on his Visa card. They headed down to the room. It had two doors, one facing the parking lot and another that led to the hallway. The motel was built on a hill, and the woods sloped away from the rear of the property.

"That was something about things going bump in the night," Alex said. "Maybe we've got ourselves a mini Overlook here."

"Overlook?"

"You know, the hotel from *The Shining*? Stephen King?"

"Never read it," Roland said. "Don't think she was talking about ghosts."

"What, then?" Alex said, taking off his coat and throwing it on one of the room's queen-sized beds.

"Wasn't going to tell you this, but I had an encounter."

"What kind of encounter?"

"You've heard of the Barker monster? Local legend, Bigfoot-type creature?"

"No, I mean, I'm familiar with Bigfoot legends. Who isn't?"

"It was outside my tent a few nights ago. At the abandoned truck stop. I ran. That's why I headed to the shelter. Scared the living crap out of me."

Alex studied him for a few moments, trying to decide if Roland was serious.

"I'm not kidding," Roland said.

"You're not drinking or anything, are you?"

"Because all homeless are drunks or druggies, right?"

Alex rolled his eyes. "That's not what I said. It's just a little tough to believe."

"It was roaming around my tent. I saw it. Plenty of people have seen it in town. It's been at people's houses and someone got killed yesterday."

"Well as long as it's not staying in the room next to us, I'm fine with it," Alex said. "I'm kind of hungry. Think I saw some vending machines near the office. You want something?"

"I'm okay for now."

"Okay, I'll be back with snacks."

Fourteen

Night began to fall outside, and Monique was at least grateful to have some sort of shelter. She'd being trying to get up the nerve to flee. She hadn't heard the creature come back. The night might provide her more cover. She wasn't sure exactly which direction to head, but if she could get a signal, she could at least call for help.

Once again, she looked out the shelter opening. Snowflakes danced around, whipped up by the wind. Not exactly inviting going out there, but it beat freezing in this shelter while she waited for that thing to return.

She wished she had her camera to at least document the experience. When she got back – and she would get back – it would make for amazing footage. She didn't want to use her phone camera, as it would deplete the battery.

Monique slipped outside. The snow stung her eyes and clung to her face. She wiped it away. Straight ahead seemed like the best option, so she fought through the deep snow. It was a damned workout.

When she was around fifty feet from the shelter, a whoop came from her left, off in the trees. She froze. Another whoop, this time from her right, answered the first. Vocalizations. She'd heard recordings of them. Some were legit recordings. Others were dubs of the original vocalizations layered over people's videos, purporting to hear Sasquatch in the woods. Fakes.

This wasn't fake. Another loud whoop. An answer, and then a third one chimed in up ahead of her.

There are more than one of them.

Had they seen her, and were they communicating somehow on her position? Leaving the shelter didn't seem like a great idea now. The deep snow would make fleeing difficult.

She managed to find her way back to the shelter. She huddled inside, shivering. Waiting.

Rodgers had to deal with the research people. The two of them were in their vehicle, parked across the street from the crime scene. He'd told them not to leave. He was considering charging them with tampering with a crime scene.

Right now, he had bigger problems. A missing woman. Monique, one of the Bigfoot researchers. A half dozen patrol vehicles were on scene. Their lights flashing, bathing the neighborhood in red and blue lights. Neighbors were out on porches or peering out windows.

Nothing he could do about it. He would send some of his guys to ask questions, knock on doors. They had a county sheriff's helicopter inbound to look for the woman. They'd be using infrared to track her heat signature.

The longer she was out there, the less chance she'd come back alive. The weather was brutal, and if that thing had her, she might already be dead.

He got a call on the radio. The chopper was inbound. Some of his guys were beating the brush. He'd instructed them not to go far. They'd spotted the thing's footprints leading away from the house, but tracking the creature could be deadly.

While he waited for the chopper, he decided to have a chat with the other two Bigfoot researchers. He knocked on their truck window and waved them out. They hopped out of the vehicle.

"What were you doing here? I specifically told your group not to mess with this type of thing."

James said, "We were going to just drive by. Monique got curious and looked at the house."

"She didn't enter," Kurt said.

"Doesn't matter. If you'd minded your own business, none of this would've happened. Did you hear or see anything?"

"Nothing," James said. "She was gone a while, so we went to check. Saw the footprints and called you all."

"There's a helicopter coming to search for her."

"You got to find her."

"We'll do our best."

Kurt said, "What about the creature?"

"We'll deal with it. My priority is finding Monique," Rodgers said.

"Are we getting charged?" Kurt said.

"As of right now, no. But if I see either of you anywhere near my crime scenes again, you'll be a guest in county lockup."

Rodgers walked away. He heard the whap of chopper rotors approaching, and then the sheriff's helicopter buzzed overhead. Ezra Richards, his K-9 officer, pulled up on the scene and parked at the curb. He got out and wrangled Trooper, his German Shepherd, from the back of the SUV.

Rodgers met them at the truck. "I'll show you where she went."

He showed Richards where the tracks started. He let Trooper sniff around, then the dog began whining and barking. Richards gave a few commands in Dutch, the language for commands. Still, the dog whined and tucked its tail. Rodgers had never seen a K-9 behave that way.

"He ever do that before?" Rodgers said.

"Never."

Richards barked a few more commands. Trooper took a few more sniffs and resumed whining. Folded his ears back. "Jesus, Lieutenant, I'm sorry."

"No need. Think he got a whiff of the creature?"

"Something's got him spooked bad."

"I don't think I'd be in a hurry to track it, either. Was hoping he could track the woman, though."

Trooper continued to mewl and looked up at Richards with sad eyes.

"Forget it," Rodgers said. "Chopper's out there anyway."

Richards gave a command and led Trooper back to the K-9 vehicle. His shoulders slumped a bit. Never seen a K-9 officer let down by his dog before.

Monique had been dozing when the helicopter buzzed overhead. At first, she thought she'd dreamt it, her mind conjuring it and giving false hope. But no, there was a chopper overhead. Were they looking for her?

She had to signal the helicopter. No way she was going to miss this opportunity. She stood up. Something in her hip cracked, and stiffness had settled into her legs and lower back. Still, she crawled to the opening and scanned the woods.

No sign of the creature. Or creatures.

She crawled out of the structure. The snow had let up a bit. That was a small favor, allowing the helicopter to fly tonight. She scanned the woods again. No sign of the Sasquatch.

The chopper swung back around and hovered, kicking up snow in a mini storm. Monique waved her arms. No doubt they'd seen her. The chopper door swung open and an officer in a flight suit lowered himself on a cable. He reached Monique and looped a harness around her, connecting the two of them.

It seemed to take an eternity for them to be lifted off the ground. She closed her eyes, waiting for an attack. But nothing came after them.

Over the rotor wash came more whoop-howls from the woods.

"Get us out of here. Hurry!"

"We're going Miss!" the crewman said. He looked up and gave a thumbs-up. The chopper's winch hauled them up, Monique belly-to-belly with the officer.

When they reached the helicopter, another crew pulled them inside, and then helped them disconnect the harness. Monique fell backward, exhausted. As she sat up, someone draped a blanket over her shoulders. She shivered as the chopper banked.

"How did you find me?" she shouted to the officer who'd rescued her.

"Infrared. We caught your heat signature. Bunch of others in the woods, too."

"I don't think they were friendly."

"Yeah, me neither."

She rode in silence as the chopper skimmed over the woods, eventually returning to the neighborhood where she'd investigated the house. It touched down in a cul-de-sac, and the officer that had rescued her helped her out of the helicopter. She saw news vans and police vehicles parked in the street.

There was also an ambulance. After scanning the street further, she spotted their truck. James and Kurt had waited here for her.

The officer said, "You should get checked out at the ambulance."

"I'm not hurt."

"Might be a good idea, anyway."

She agreed, and he escorted her to the ambulance. She spotted James running over. He embraced her, kissed the top of Monique's head.

"Glad you're okay. You hurt?"

"Just freezing cold and tired," she said.

Kurt joined them. "Jesus, you scared the crap out of us."

She broke off the embrace. "It happened fast. Damn thing snatched me up and ran off."

"Where did it take you?" Kurt said.

"Out in the damned woods. Wound up in some sort of stick and twig shelter. Don't know what it wanted with me."

"We're just glad you're back," James said. "No more going off on your own."

"I don't need a babysitter."

An EMT poked his head out the rear of the ambulance. "Let's have a look at you."

Monique climbed in the ambulance and sat on the bench. The EMT took her vitals and asked her some questions. She told him she had no injuries. He offered to take her to the hospital if she wanted, but she declined. After the check-up, she brushed past a group of reports, who were waiting nearby. She put her hand up, waved them off.

Along with Kurt and James, she made it back to the truck, where a police detective waited. She was tall and slim, with intense, dark eyes.

"Monique, I'm Detective Perez."

"I'm tired, detective."

"Just a moment of your time."

"Can we do this in the morning?"

"Tell me quick what happened and I'll get out of your hair."

"I was checking out the house. Heard a noise, then it snatched me up and ran off with me."

"What snatched you?" Perez said.

"A Sasquatch."

She studied Perez's face for a moment, looking for any sign of disbelief. Her expression was grim.

"What were you doing at the house?"

"Just shooting some footage. We're with a Bigfoot research team. I didn't bust in or anything."

"It's still a crime scene."

"Am I being charged with anything?"

"Not at this time. It was an animal that took you?"

"Wasn't a man, that's for sure. Can I get going now?"

"You're staying at the Bear Lodge outside town?"

Monique said, "That's right."

"I'll follow up if I need anything," Perez said, and walked away muttering something about a monster hunt.

"Let's get you back to the hotel," James said.

"Don't need a babysitter. I'm fine."

"I wasn't saying that."

"Quit taking my temperature," Monique said.

She slipped into the truck, waiting for James to get behind the wheel. He was concerned, and that was sweet, but she didn't need coddling. She'd just survived a damned Sasquatch kidnapping, after all. Maybe she was being a bitch. James was just concerned, and she was being too hard on him. Some rest might help her mood.

He and Kurt got in and they pulled away.

Fifteen

Gina lay in bed, unable to sleep. She'd heard a helicopter in the distance. The incident with the rock throwing had left her edgy. The police had vacated, and all that remained outside was the ruined SUV. Steve snored next to her. Nothing disrupted that man's sleep. He once napped while roofers worked on their house, pounding and scraping off shingles.

She had the semiautomatic in the nightstand. Steve had the shotgun propped in the corner for easy access. They were going to leave in the morning, all four of them. She decided that. The snow had abated. An Uber could take them to a hotel. From there, they'd get home somehow.

And if no one else was on board, they could stay here. Just being in the lodge made her uneasy. What if that thing were lurking around right now, searching for a way in, waiting to attack them?

She hopped out of bed and sat in one of the suite's armchairs. Steve rolled onto his side. One arm flopped over the edge of the mattress. Still sound asleep.

Bored and restless, she grabbed the novel she'd been reading from her bag. It was tough to focus, and she had to keep re-reading passages. After fifteen minutes, she set the book down and looked out the window, which overlooked the woods.

Snow clung to the pines in clumps. The sky was a blue-gray, full of clouds. It would be nice to see a star or two, or even the moon. Somehow it would provide hope. But it was like looking at a piece of slate.

She was tempted to wake Steve up to keep her company, but that wasn't fair. Being alone in the middle of the night with a head full of worries was the worst feeling in the world.

Maybe a hot shower would tire her out. She grabbed her robe and headed to the adjoining bathroom. She didn't dare look out the window this time. Instead, she reached in the shower and turned it on. Disrobed, then kicked her clothes aside. From the vanity top, she grabbed a hair scrunchie and tied up in a messy bun. When it was good and steamy, she stepped in the shower.

She let the multiple shower heads pour hot water on her. Closed her eyes and leaned her head back. The water felt incredible, and the knots in her shoulders began to melt.

Her relaxation was cut short by the massive roar that came from outside. She shut the water off and stood listening.

After a moment, she stepped out of the shower and grabbed a towel. Dried off in a hurry and slipped into the robe.

A long whoop echoed outside. A series of cries answered it. It sounded like multiple creatures. Steve banged on the bathroom door. "You in there?"

Gina opened the door.

"You hear that?"

"It's why I cut my shower short."

"Sounds like a bunch of them out there."

She scooped up her clothes and returned to the bedroom, where she got dressed, throwing on her outfit from earlier. Steve grabbed the shotgun and looked out the window.

"You guys in there?" Priya said from the hallway.

"Come on in," Gina said.

Priya entered, dressed in a baggy t-shirt and plaid lounge pants. "What now? There were a bunch of howls."

"Not sure how close they were," Steve said.

David joined them in the bedroom. He ran a hand through his close-cropped hair. He looked like a man who was about to play Russian routlette.

"We can't even get out of here. Stuck," David said.

"Everything's locked up," Steve said.

More howls tore through the woods. It sounded like they were getting closer to the lodge. Steve was still looking out the window. "See anything?"

"Nothing," Steve said.

Gina grabbed the semiautomatic from the nightstand. She headed to the bathroom. As much as she dreaded looking out the window again, they had to keep an eye on things. A look out the bathroom window showed no sign of the creature.

She felt helpless. All they could do was wait. At least they were armed.

The four of them headed downstairs to have a look. Gina checked the rear doors. The deck spotlight didn't reveal anything. While she looked out back, David and Steve went around looking out the other windows. Priya meandered over to the French doors, joining Gina.

"Anything?"

"They must be in the woods."

"Should we call the cops again?" Priya said.

"Well, they haven't come close yet."

They gathered near the sectional in the living room.

"We should find a way out of here at first light. Got to be a way to get a ride," Gina said. "I'm not waiting to see what happens."

"She's right," Priya said. "I say we cut our losses."

"We go to the hotel then?" Steve said.

"What about our vehicle? Not sure how you go about getting a boulder removed from your car," David said.

"We'll worry about that later. Not waiting for something to come barging in here and murder us," Priya said.

"So we keep watch for tonight and leave in the morning?" Gina said.

They all agreed on that. Priya offered to put on a pot of coffee. That sounded good to Gina. Couldn't sleep anyways. Might as well dose up on caffeine. As Priya grabbed the ground coffee from the cupboard, she shrieked.

A shadow fell across the kitchen.

Something was on the back deck.

Jesse didn't sleep well anymore. Hadn't since he'd become a widower. Most nights, he puttered around at all hours, sometimes reading, other times combing the streaming services for a movie that wasn't crap.

He didn't want to tell Tim, but Jesse was worried about going back home. Sure, he'd have a new door, but what if that thing came back and didn't leave this time? It had been nice spending time here with Brian and Tim. Last night, they'd played Scrabble at Jesse's request.

For a bit, it felt like when Tim was young and they had family game nights or headed to the Aurora for a movie. He supposed he was an old fool hanging onto the past. Couldn't stay with his son and son-in-law forever.

Unable to sleep, he took out Dad's journal again. There were a few pages of pencil sketches. The lake and some trees. A sketch of a trout. The drawings weren't half-bad. He'd never witness his father draw, only viewed the rough sketches he'd done in the journal. The entries picked up again after the sketches.

Last night was a little tense. I guess I drifted off sometime after ten. That's when I got woken up. I heard footsteps just outside the tent. Crushing leaves and sticks. There was a smell like an open septic tank. I think whatever was out there got pretty close to the tent.

I just laid there and listened. Heartbeat was definitely going over the edge. It came close a few times. I heard it sniffing around and I laid there, nice and still. Eventually, it trailed off into the woods. After I have my breakfast this morning, I'm going to move camp.

I had breakfast and broke down the tent. I happened to take a look around. There were a lot of branches broken. Something big beat a trail through the brush. Thinking it must have been a bear. I'm glad to be moving the tent.

I moved to a spot around the other side of the lake. Found a nice little place. We'll try this again tonight.

I'm settled in. Sitting here and eating lunch. Nice little spot right by the lake. Think I'll try some fishing in a bit. This spot is better, but I still feel like I'm being watched. I'm probably just spooked from last night. Still a little hinky to me, but things will be fine.

I decided to take a hike. Things got strange. I got the sense something was following me off to the left. In the brush. I would stop. It would stop. Could be an animal stalking me. Mountain lion? Maybe a bear? It trailed off when I returned to camp. Might give this one more night then head back. Don't want to end up as something's lunch.

Most of the afternoon was quiet. Sat by the lake here and just took things in. Sipped a few beers. Then some odd things happened again. A rock came flying into camp. It rolled near my feet before bouncing into the lake. I got up and looked around. There was no one to be seen. I hollered a warning to whoever threw the rock. Probably some wise guy kids running around and playing jokes.

Wouldn't have been a joke if it conked me on my coconut. Two more rocks came sailing into camp. One was the size of a football, and it threw up dirt when it hit the ground. That one would've been the end of me had it hit me. Looked around again and didn't see anyone.

It's obvious someone doesn't want me here. It's getting a little dark to hike out now, so I'll wait until morning. Hoping I don't have more visitors tonight. I don't feel much like fishing, so I'll pop open a can of beans and have that for dinner. It isn't gourmet, but I don't want to be distracted fishing with some rock-throwing moron out in the woods.

There were a few more sketches. This time, one of the lake and some separate drawings of pines, which Dad had labeled *Tree Studies* in his messy handwriting. The drawings made him wonder about his father. Sometimes Dad would sit and stare, his mind off somewhere. He would seem sad. Whenever someone asked him what was wrong, he'd say "Nothing. Wheels are just turning."

Had his father wanted to be an artist? Or something other than a factory worker. Maybe that was the reason for the melancholy demeanor. Jesse never would've asked him. They just didn't have conversations like that. Dad usually asked him how school was. They would talk baseball and if the Yankees would get to the World Series again. But never about hopes and dreams.

Jesse closed the journal for now. From reading it in the past, he knew there was a bit more about the camping trip. The part he suspected Dad never wanted to discuss.

He put the journal back in the drawer. Going back to the house weighed on his mind. At least he'd have Rosco with him. He was a good watchdog and could warn Jesse of approaching danger.

Still wasn't going to help him sleep, though.

Sixteen

Priya was frozen in the kitchen, holding the coffee pot. Gina waved, indicating Priya should get away from the doors. Gina heard the thumping on the deck. She went and grabbed Priya by the arm, dragging her from the kitchen.

David killed the lights downstairs. The creature on the deck came into view. Its head was out of sight. A massive, furry body passed in front of the doors. The beast let out a low growl. Gina got in a shooter's stance, aiming at the door.

Steve racked the shotgun. He aimed at the rear doors, as well. The creature stopped and lowered its head, peering through the glass. It had red eyes. Seemed to be looking Gina in the eye. It bared its teeth, revealing nasty-looking canines.

Gina flipped off the safety. The creature grunted, its breath fogging the glass.

"What the hell does it want?" David said.

"I don't know, go ask it," Steve said.

"Shut up, jackass" David said.

No one laughed. The creature remained at the door, peering in at them. Gina felt like she was being jolted with tiny electric shocks. She would swear the creature was thinking, plotting. There was an intelligence behind those eyes.

They watched it. The monster chuffed. As they watched the Sasquatch peering at them, the front door exploded inward. A second Sasquatch burst into the lodge. Steve whirled and fired. The buckshot struck the beast in the shoulder. It roared in anger and bared down on Steve.

He racked the gun again, but the beast swatted him against the wall. His skull made a sickening crack and he dropped the gun. Steve hit the ground and began twitching. Gina screamed.

Priya ducked around the kitchen counter. Steve lay on the ground. A bloody splotch stained the wall from where his head hit. David tried to run. The Sasquatch thumped him on the back. Bone crunched. David fell forward, face smacking the hardwood with a sound like someone squashing rotten fruit.

Gina took aim and fired two rounds into the beast's back. It spun and charged her. Before she could fire again, it bashed her arm, and the gun flew from her hand. It scooped her up in a bear hug and lifted her off the ground.

It ran for the front door, squeezing through the opening. She banged her shins on the door frame as it ran with her. She wiggled. Couldn't move an inch.

The creature rushed her outside. Moving fast now, the beast taking long strides. It bore her into the woods. Branches scratched her head and face. She screamed for help, watching the lodge diminish behind her. The darkness enveloped her as they moved deeper into the woods.

She thought about the blood stain on the wall. Steve's head had smashed against the paneling. He wasn't moving, last she saw. It had all gone so badly, so quickly.

Gina tried to wiggle free, but there was no escaping the creature's grip. It grunted as it carried her away. She would run the first chance she got. Better to freeze to death out here than die at the hands of a monster.

Noah Mendez parked his Honda in the driveway behind his father's truck. He'd barely gotten it through the snow piled up in the driveway. Looked like the plow guy hadn't been by yet. Noah hoped he would come, as snowblowing would fall on him if the plow guy stiffed.

His head spun a bit. He'd had a few too many beers down at Brewster Public House. Along with Darrel and Katie, they'd closed the place down, sticking around until last call. He probably shouldn't have driven. Nearly rear-ended a snowplow on the way home.

If he was lucky, Dad would be in bed and wouldn't notice the beer on his breath. Or the staggering. He slogged through the snow, which immediately wound up in his sneakers. Should've worn boots. Idiot.

The spotlight wasn't on, either, leaving the driveway in darkness. As he approached the garage, he was aware of something standing off to his left, just to the side of the garage. A low growl came from its throat.

Those were the same noises they'd been hearing for weeks. Dad blew it off, saying it was a bear or something.

A jolt of fear shot through his guts. "Who's there?"

The huge thing stepped closer. It had to be seven or eight feet tall. It was a monster movie special. The beast bared its teeth. The reddish eyes bored into him. His bladder was full and he felt warm piss run down his leg.

The creature grabbed him and snatched him off his feet. He let out a sharp yell, but he doubted anyone in the house heard him.

Gina found herself in a dome constructed of sticks and leaves. She was freezing cold. She shivered in the confines of the structure. The Sasquatch had shoved her along, urging her inside. Once she was in, it had wandered off into the woods.

After she'd been in the structure for about an hour, she heard it crashing through the brush. She heard a man screaming and yelling. He sounded panicked, as was expected.

Gina inched to the shelter's opening. The creature approached, a man of around twenty-five locked in its arms. The Sasquatch threw the man on the ground near the shelter's opening. It nudged him, and he rolled near the opening, crawling in as the creature advanced on him.

He scrambled on hands and knees, clearing the opening. The beast crashed off again.

She could smell beer fumes coming off him.

"Jesus, that was something," the kid said.

"What's your name?"

"Noah. Who are you?"

"Gina. Where did it grab you?"

"In my driveway. We'd been hearing noises in the woods for a few weeks. Guess I know what it was, now. Why are you here?"

"I got an invitation."

"Seriously, what happened?" Noah said.

"They attacked our lodge. It broke down the front door, carried me off."

"Damn," Noah said. "Wonder why it brought us here?"

"They. There are more than one."

Noah rubbed his hands together. "Jesus, it's cold. You don't have a coat?"

"I was in the living room when it busted in."

"Here," Noah said, removing his coat. "We can take turns wearing it."

He handed the coat to her. It smelled greasy, like he'd been around fried food, but she wasn't going to decline. She slipped the coat on and zipped it.

"We have to get out of here," she said.

"How? Don't think it's going to let us walk away."

"Run and head for somewhere safe. I know the direction back to the lodge where I was staying."

"I live in town. Jesus, what do you think it wants with us?"

"I'm not sticking around to find out," Gina said. She crawled to the opening and looked out. There was no sign of the creature. As she inched out of the opening, a roar bellowed from the woods. She couldn't see it, but the beast could see her.

She backed inside. This wasn't going to be easy.

At first light, the snow kicked up again. Gina and Noah had shared the jacket, each wearing it for fifteen minutes at a time. She found out he was a political science major at Buffalo State University. He'd been out drinking with some classmates, and upon returning, the creature had snatched him. Because his parents were in bed, no one had seen the abduction, although they would've reported him missing by now.

She heard crunching in the snow. She looked out and saw one of the large Sasquatch approaching. It came up to the structure. Gina backed against the wall. Noah scooted closer to her. He had a look of terror on his face.

The creature shook the structure. Dried leaves and snow filtered down on their heads. It growled and intensified the thrashing. Leaves and bits of dirt fell on their heads.

The creature smashed a fist through the top of the dome. Noah gave a cry.

"Come on. Not going to die sitting here," she said, and tugged his arm, pulling him along as the Sasquatch smashed in the roof. Why would it stick them inside and then destroy the makeshift dome?

As she scurried through the snow, Gina glanced at the Sasquatch. It stood with its long arms at its side, glaring at them.

"I think it wanted us out of there," Gina said.

"No kidding."

"I mean, for a reason. Why isn't it coming after us?"

"Who cares?" Let's go."

Gina scanned the woods. The lodge was to the south, down the slope. At least she thought that was the way. "Follow me."

They started down the slope, Gina looking back at the creature, which had taken a few steps, but wasn't chasing them. She and Noah picked up speed, trudging through deep snow. The wind ripped through her. Noah had the coat on. The lodge had better be nearby. If not, exposure might kill her before the Sasquatch could.

Gina looked back again. Nothing following. Maybe it was letting them go, for whatever reason. They slogged ahead. Her lungs were scorched. Damn, this was hard going.

"We're never going to make it," Noah said, and right after the words came out, he puked a stream of yellow vomit into the snow. Gina wrinkled her nose. Recycled hops.

"Suck it up and keep going."

Noah wiped his mouth and groaned. He still had some puke on his chin after wiping.

"Clean off the rest of your mouth," Gina said.

"Sorry, focused on not getting killed."

Howls came from the left and the right. They sounded close. She should've known escape wouldn't be easy. She sensed movement to the left. Out of the woods came a Sasquatch, this one not as large and broad as the others. Dark gray fur. It was between six and six-five.

An adolescent? It approached, sniffing the air. A second creature came from the right, closer to Noah. Another adolescent, slimmer and shorter than the adult. It looked no less fierce. It growled at them. They wouldn't have a chance out here with no weapons.

"Shit," Noah said. A look of panic crossed his face and he bolted, high-stepping through the snow. After ten feet, he stumbled and rolled down the ridge. The young creatures bounded after him.

It dawned on Gina that they were being used as prey for the younger creatures. That's why they'd been kept alive.

The nearer creature pounced on Noah's back. It bit down on his skull. The bone crunched. Noah's right eye popped from the socket. He screamed, his voice rising to a terrible pitch and echoing over the hills.

Noah struggled under the creature's weight. It pinned his arms down. The second creature reached him, grabbed his arm, and bit down on his hand. It took off his pinky and forth finger, leaving jagged stumps. The blood stained the fresh snow.

The creature bent his arm back against his torso. A pop filled the air and he screamed again. The creature that was on his back stood up and began jumping up and down on Noah, stomping him into the snow.

Gina cringed. They seemed to be intent on inflicting the most amount of pain possible. She also took this as her opportunity to run. Nothing she could do to help Noah.

She plowed downhill, legs pumping, heart slamming in her chest. From behind her, Noah's screams had died down to whimpers. She looked back and saw one of the adolescents gnawing on Noah's severed arm.

Gina reached the bottom of the ridge. A loud whoop came from the top of the hill, and she spotted one of the adolescents. The fur around its mouth was slicked with blood.

She wouldn't outrun it, even if there wasn't deep snow. She looked around, frantic. In the side of the hill she spotted an opening, possibly the entrance to a small cave. It looked big enough for her to shimmy inside.

The creature started down the hill. She ducked her head and shoulders inside the opening and began to scoot. For a moment, she thought she was stuck, leaving the lower half of her vulnerable to the Sasquatch. She wiggled and squirmed, slipping through the opening and dropping a few feet to the ground.

The Sasquatch was now right outside the cave, crunching ice and snow. Gray light filtered in the opening. Still, mostly darkness enveloped her. She backed away from the hole. Heard the creature sniffing around for her.

She willed herself to be quiet. This would be the worst possible time for a cough or sneeze. Despite her silence, the creature located her and peered in the hole. She backed away from the opening and pressed against the sharp rock.

At least it can't fit in here.

It growled at her. She could smell its rank breath filtering into the opening. It reached inside, but came up short. She skittered sideways, and found a small alcove, this one large enough to crouch inside. She tucked herself in.

The creature grumbled, then yanked its arm out. It gave an angry roar and she heard it go stomping off. Cool air blew from farther in the cave. The alcove she was hiding in continued deeper under the hill.

With no light and no caving experience, going deeper in the cave would be suicidal. She'd wait it out here. When it was safe, she'd try and make a run for it. Maybe the monsters would get bored and give up, although she was still in their territory.

A shiver passed through her. She couldn't remain here long. Noah had been wearing the coat. *He doesn't need it anymore.* She wished for the coat, then felt a stab of guilt. The kid had died horribly, and all she could think about was his coat.

The same would happen to her if she didn't get away.

Seventeen

Back out to the goddamned lodge again. Rodgers pulled into the driveway in the middle of the night. Two of his patrol vehicles were on scene, along with two ambulances. The EMTs were rushing one guy on a gurney into the back of a rig. They brought the second patient out, and the attractive Indian woman he'd seen before was with the man. He guessed it was her husband.

They loaded the second guy up and the rigs pulled out, lights going. One of them fired up their siren and it screamed away. Rodgers spotted Schwartz by the open front door.

He had a search team and more officers headed to the scene. One of the women had been grabbed and carried off. The second one in less than twenty-four hours. The chopper was also on the way. He hoped for a quick recovery, like the last woman they'd found in the woods.

He approached Schwartz. "What's the word?"

"That first guy they took out, he got it worst. Likely a fractured skull. The other guy wasn't moving. According to his wife, Priya, it thumped him pretty hard."

"Who'd it carry off?"

"Gina Peretti. Married to the guy with the fractured skull, Steven Peretti."

"She's the one I dealt with earlier. Perez on the case?"

"She was here. Heading to the hospital to get a statement from Priya."

Rodgers stepped inside. They'd have to get statements from the witnesses. Blood had been splashed on the wall. Smeared on the floor. The animal stench of the creature still lingered in the air. They were going to have to hunt it down and kill it. No question.

They should've left. He should've forced them. Found them a ride somehow. This was a goddamned mess, and he felt partly to blame.

Rodgers headed home as the sun was breaking over the horizon. The sky had cleared some, and slices of pink sunrise were visible. Maybe they'd get some sunshine today, although the weather was calling for more snow tonight. Lake effect bands, one to two inches per hour.

The chopper and search parties were still out looking for the Peretti woman. He was going to stop home for a quick shower and bite to eat, then head to the station.

As he pulled into the driveway, his cell rang. It was Perez.

"Hey, got a minute?" she said.

"Go ahead."

"I followed up with the other vic at the the hospital. Priya?"

"What'd you find out?"

"They'd been hearing noises for a while. They all gathered downstairs. That's when they heard something on the deck. It gets wilder from there. You ready for this?"

"Try me."

"One of those things looks in the rear doors. They freak out. Then another one busts in and grabs the Peretti woman. Oh, and messes up the guys pretty bad. The one guy had a busted skull and a brain bleed. The other one's got two fractured vertebrae."

"Son of a bitch."

Perez said, "Did you ever think we'd be dealing with something like this?"

"Not to this extent. I mean, we got the occasional sighting or thing going bump in the night, but no."

"It's all over the goddamned news. Channel Four is calling Barker Bigfoot Central or some stupid shit like that."

Rodgers sighed. After the chief, he was now the highest ranking officer of Bigfoot, USA. Not only was that a title he didn't need, but they still had a problem. It had killed someone, maimed others, and a woman was missing. Who the hell did you call to hunt down a

Sasquatch? Brody hired Quint to handle his shark problem. Was there someone like that for cryptids? "I'm sure they're taking the story and running with it."

"Got to admit, it's huge."

"Is that a Bigfoot pun?"

"Guess it could be, but no. That's all I got for now."

"Keep me posted."

They ended the call. Rodgers parked and headed inside. The house was dark, and when he cruised by the girls' rooms, their doors were closed. Sunday morning. They wouldn't be up before ten or eleven.

He headed to the kitchen, put on a pot of coffee. Then he took a quick shower and changed into a fresh uniform. After heading into the kitchen, he made some instant oatmeal and slugged down a glass of milk with it.

Allie shuffled into the kitchen, dressed in lounge pants and a baggy t-shirt. Big, fuzzy socks on her feet.

"You rose from your tomb this early?" Rodgers said.

"I heard someone out here. Glad it wasn't a burglar. I would've had to hurt them."

"Everything okay here? Quiet while I was gone?"

"Like an empty church. What was your call about?"

"Woman got snatched up at the log house on seventy-eight. Two other people injured."

"The Barker monster strike again?"

"It did," Rodgers said, stirring his oatmeal.

"What are you doing about it?"

"We've got to go looking for it. Or should I say, them. Witness reported more than one of them at the log house."

"More than one?" Allie said.

Rodgers nodded. "Just keeps getting better. I have to head back out."

"You just got home."

"You and your sister will have to hold down the fort. It's all hands on deck until we get this solved. You two are to stay put, understand?"

"I wanted to go to Morgan's and hang out," Allie said.

"That's a negative."

"This sucks."

"Agreed, but my job is to-"

"Keep us safe."

"See? You know the drill."

"Going back to bed now. Be careful out there, Dad."

"Will do."

Gina couldn't stay in the cave. It wasn't quite as cold as outside, but she'd still shivered for hours. Hypothermia might get her if the monsters didn't. She crawled to the opening and listened. Hadn't heard them for a while.

She took a risk and poked her head out the opening. No sign of the creatures. The snow had stopped. A bit of sunshine poked through the clouds. This might be the best chance she would get to escape.

After wiggling out of the opening, she got to her feet. Started heading in the general direction of the lodge. Would the police be looking for her? Staying in one spot when lost increased your chances of being found, but she was ill-equipped for the cold. Plus, those things were running around.

She climbed back up the ridge, a light sweat forming on her skin despite the cold. Noah's body was gone, leaving only blood-tinged snow and one boot. God only knew what they did with his corpse.

The domelike structure had been demolished. Broken sticks and leaves littered the ground. The creature had been thorough in ruining it. She moved on, heading in the direction of the lodge.

After she'd gone a few hundred yards, she caught movement to her right. She froze. A deer bounded through the woods.

"Scared me, you son of a bitch," she muttered.

She heard something else in the distance: a helicopter buzzing. Were they searching for her? She had to be a few miles at least from the cabin. Would they be checking this area?

The helicopter buzzed overhead. She looked up and waved her arms.

"Thank Christ," she said.

For a moment, she thought it didn't see her, but it circled back around and began to hover. The door opened and she saw a crewman in an olive jumpsuit looking down at her.

A deep roar erupted from the woods. It came from back down the ridge. They were close. Maybe the helicopter had attracted them. She looked up. The crewman was lowering himself down on a cable. They were going to pull her up.

She waved and pointed at the ridge. "They're coming! Hurry up!"

The crewman either ignored her or couldn't hear over the din of the chopper. He continued his descent. Another roar. This time it was closer. Sounded like they were coming up the ridge.

The helicopter crewman dangled ten feet above. Gina turned and saw a huge Sasquatch charging over the ridge. The crewman spotted it and shouted something into his headset mic. As the crewman almost reached Gina, the Sasquatch lunged. She ducked and rolled in the snow.

It grabbed hold of the crewman's legs and yanked. Gina heard a pop. The guy screamed as the Sasquatch pulled him down farther. Up above, the helicopter swayed from the tugging on the line.

The damn thing was strong. The crewman was attached by a harness and carabiners. The beast gave a tug, and the crewman broke free, ending up in the Sasquatch's arms. It squeezed him in a massive hug. His helmet fell off. A weak groan escaped him.

Gina heard his ribs snap, and a glob of blood splattered from his mouth, staining the creature's fur. From above, another crewman leaned out the door. He took aim with a pistol and fired down at the creature. The rounds punched into the snow, missing the creature.

The Sasquatch flung the broken crewman against a tree, his back cracking against the trunk. He fell motionless into the snow. The Bigfoot roared up at the chopper. A round slammed into its chest.

This was her chance to run. It was distracted.

She broke into a run. She hoped her sense of direction was good. It had to be this way. At least she thought.

More gunfire erupted from above, a series of shots echoing through the woods. Gina glanced at the creature. It staggered backwards, swatting at the air as if surrounded by stinging insects.

More shots rained down, and the creature bounded away, disappearing down the ridge.

She pushed ahead, fighting the snow, determined to escape.

Eighteen

About forty minutes later, she breathed a sigh of relief when she spotted the lodge's roof through the trees. She paused for a moment at the wood's edge, watching the cabin. There was no sign of anyone. No animal stench of the creature.

She crept to the front door, which was partially open. Snow had blown into the entryway. Gina slipped inside. She spotted the blood stain on the wall and a lump formed in her throat. Steve had been hurled against the wall. She had to find out if he was okay.

"Hello?" she called.

No answer.

The semiautomatic was lying on the counter. She'd dropped it when the creature grabbed her. Small favor that it was still here. She grabbed it and headed upstairs. She heard the helicopter off in the distance. The police were probably swarming to the spot where the crewman had been killed.

She slipped into the bedroom and found her phone. It still had a good charge on it. She called nine-one-one and told them who she was. They were going to send a patrol vehicle right away.

Gina went back downstairs. She needed answers right away about Steve and the others. She tried his cell, but it went right to voicemail.

Check your missed calls.

She had three missed calls, all from the same number. *Huntington County Medical Center.*

Gina dialed. A woman answered after a few rings.

"ICU, this is Lisa."

"I'm Gina Peretti. I had calls from this number. I think my husband Steve was brought in."

"I'm glad you called. Your husband was able to give us your number."

"How is Steve?"

"He's resting comfortably. He had a fractured skull and a brain bleed. They did emergency surgery and he's doing well. Dr. Lang can tell you more. He did the surgery."

"Can I see him?"

"Of course. Ninth floor. He's in Nine-Nineteen. Anything else?"

"No. I'll be up as soon as I get a ride."

She thanked the nurse and ended the call. An engine cut out in the driveway. Emergency lights flashed. She went to the door and looked out to see a Barker patrol vehicle parked behind the Jeep. The officer approached the door. "Are you hurt?"

"Just freezing cold."

"Are you the only one here?"

"Yeah. That thing killed one of the helicopter crew. They were trying to rescue me."

"I heard the chatter. Let's get you out of here. Not safe," the officer said.

"Can you take me to Huntington County? My husband's in ICU."

"I can drop you off."

The plan had changed. Rodgers got a call that a state trooper on the chopper got killed. The Barker monster was responsible. The woman – Gina Peretti – had escaped. She was with her husband at Huntington General. He pulled up near the lodge on Route 78. A combination of state police vehicles and Barker PD were parked along the road.

Some of the state police were unloading ATVs and snowmobiles from a trailer. The mood seemed somber. Groups of the state guys gathered in clusters, spoke in low tones. They'd lost one of their own. Rodgers had never lost an officer, but he'd been to some funerals for his fellow police. He felt for those guys.

He supposed he'd better get ready. As the highest-ranking cop, he wanted to go represent the department. The chief had given him the okay. Plus, he wanted a part in ending the damn thing's life. It wasn't a legend anymore. People had died because of that damned thing.

In his patrol SUV, Rodgers put on heavy boots. He grabbed his twelve gauge and went to find his counterpart in the state police. He found the guy, Major Bradford. He had the standard military cut favored by the state cops. His ruddy cheeks were chafed red by the icy winds.

Rodgers introduced himself.

"You've seen this thing?" Bradford said.

"Yeah, it's big and nasty. And there's more than one."

"Just so we're clear, we're going to kill it?"

"That's the plan."

"I don't want PETA or some animal-loving group coming after us."

"I don't think PETA covers Sasquatches."

That got a laugh from Bradford. "This is nuts. A goddamn Bigfoot. Suppose I'll have a good story to tell. You want to ride on the ATV with me? We'll follow a trail up there."

The ATV looked like a small tank. An armored ski-patrol vehicle. It had treads and an enclosed cab. Dark gray paint and the state police insignia painted on the side. There appeared to be enough room for four men in the cab. "Sounds good."

"The chopper's going to act as a spotter for us. Going to recover our guy up there."

"Damn shame about that," Rodgers said.

"I had to call his family. Four kids and a wife left behind."

The state guys had the snowmobiles and a second ATV unloaded. Looked like they'd be taking the two ATVs and three snowmobiles up the hill.

"Looks like we're ready," Bradford said.

He followed Bradford to the ATV and they piled in the back. Two guys hopped in the front and the driver started it up. They lurched forward and started up a trail into the hills.

The ATV slowed, the treads squealing like a tank in an old war movie. Overhead, the chopper buzzed. Rodgers spotted the crewman, or what was left of him. His chest was flattened, as if a large boulder had landed on him. Blood stained the snow all around him and covered his face like some odd warpaint. His arm was also bent back at the elbow. Looked like it had been snapped at a bad angle.

The second ATV pulled up, as did the police on snowmobiles. The helicopter had radioed Bradford a few times. No sighting of the creature so far.

Because the first helicopter had its winch system damaged, they'd brought in a second one from upstate. The helicopter hovered overhead. A few of the state police approached the dead officer, a body bag in hand. They set the bag on the ground. Rodgers looked away for the next part, thinking he'd offer the dead some respect.

When he looked back, the downed officer had been zipped in the bag. The chopper lowered a stretcher basket and the officers strapped the body in. The body was hauled up, spinning in the wind. The crew eased it into the chopper and it began circling the area.

As soon as the chopper left, he heard the first howl. It came from down a ridge to the left. The troopers drew their guns. One other officer had a shotgun. Rodgers pointed his weapon in the direction of the ridge.

Bradford said, "What the hell?"

A second howl, sounding somehow mournful, carried from the opposite direction. Bradford radioed the chopper and said, "You have a visual on anything?"

"Two large shapes. Moving toward you," the pilot said.

"How far?"

"Fifty yards, max."

Rodgers turned away from the ridge and scanned the woods. It was damned dark in there. The shadows had shadows. This time, a roar shook Rodgers. He wanted to get in the ATV and haul ass out of here. That wouldn't solve the problem.

Maybe we should've called in the National Guard.

He spotted the first creature. It approached, taking long strides. Covered in black and gray matted fur. The one next to it had dark brown fur. Both creatures appeared to be over seven feet tall and were thick as redwood trees.

The dark brown Sasquatch threw its head back and roared. Both Sasquatches charged. Rodgers fired, as did Bradford.

"They're coming from both directions!" Bradford said.

Rodgers glanced at the top of the ridge. Two smaller, slighter creatures bore down on them. They looked like juveniles. No less ferocious. They came with bared teeth and wild, red eyes. Two of Bradford's men opened fire on the smaller creatures. They howled in anger as the rounds slammed into them.

Rodgers looked back. The two larger beasts entered the clearing. He blasted the brownish one. It reared back, the shot ripping into its arm. Bradford peeled off a few shots at the darker Sasquatch. It reached him, swatting his head. Rodgers heard a sharp crack, and Bradford fell dead in the snow, his head twisted at a horrific angle.

Behind him, semiautomatics popped. The larger Sasquatch turned on Rodgers. It bore down on him, teeth bared. Before he could rack the gun, it bashed him in the chest. He flew backward into the snow. Felt like a mini wrecking ball had slammed into him.

He heard a howl of pain behind him. Looked up as the two larger Sasquatches moved passed him. For some reason, they weren't interested in him. He turned his head.

Bradford's men had downed one of the younger creatures. It lay on its back in the snow, blood matting its fur. The darker Bigfoot grabbed the nearest guy by the head, slapping two enormous hands on either side of his skull. It yanked upward. Something snapped in his neck, and the man's eyes rolled back in his head. The creature dropped him in the snow.

The brown Sasquatch pounced on a second man, biting into his neck. A geyser of blood splattered the creatures face. The blood steamed in the cold air.

Rodgers turned his head. The shotgun lay a few feet away. He rolled on his side. Jolts of pain shot through his chest and ribcage. It felt like the monster had busted something in him. Wincing, he rolled over and crawled toward the gun.

Behind him, horrible, high-pitched screams came from the men. Gunshots rang out. The smell of shit filled the air as dying men's bowels gave way. The stench from the creatures mixed with the smells of death, churning Rodgers' stomach.

The screams and gunshots cut out. Rodgers kept still in the snow. His initial desire to grab the shotgun would lead to death. He was sure the other officers had perished. He rested his head in the snow and remained quiet.

His back was to the creatures. He heard them grunting, and then the two larger ones gave a bone-rattling roar. Rodgers squeezed his eyes shut. He was sure they were going to kill him.

One of the beasts made a low, whimpering sound unlike the fierce roars and howls he'd heard before. He heard their footsteps in the snow.

Stay still. Maybe they'll think you're dead.

He opened one eye. The larger, darker Sasquatch passed by with the dead juvenile cradled in its arms. The dark brown creature and the other younger Sasquatch followed. They headed into the woods and their footsteps grew faint.

When he was sure they'd gone, he sat up, fiery pain rocketing through his chest. He managed to crawl and grab the shotgun. The helicopter circled back over. His radio crackled.

"What the hell happened?"

"Officers down. They just about wiped us out. I need help. They busted me up."

"Sending help."

"You see them?" Rodgers said.

"Negative. Hold tight."

Rodgers figured the creatures had headed into the thick brush and trees. They had failed. He lay back down, the shotgun draped across his chest. Each breath was an agony.

Hopefully the creatures wouldn't be back before they got him off the hill.

Nineteen

Back home, Rodgers lay on the couch. He had two fractured ribs and a bruised sternum. Nothing they could do for the ribs. He was to take it easy. They didn't even wrap the ribs. The ER doc told him they don't like to do that. Compresses things and messes with breathing. They worry about pneumonia setting in.

Allie had picked him up from the hospital. He'd given her permission to drive under the circumstances. She was in the kitchen making him a cup of tea.

"Two sugars Dad?"

"Please."

She entered the living room with his favorite mug. Some of the lettering had faded, but it read *World's Greatest Dad*. They'd gotten it for him when they were little. Allie handed him the mug of steaming English Breakfast Tea.

Rodgers looked out the bay window. Night had fallen, and the snow began to whip around. It always felt like an alien landscape out there in the dark of winter. As if he were a pilot on a downed starship stranded on a strange world. He'd be glad for sunlight and spring, although that seemed far off.

"How are the ribs?"

"Call me Everlast because I feel like a punching bag."

"Ha ha. You should take your painkiller after you have your tea."

"Hate those damned things. They make me loopy."

He'd been on Vicodin after a wisdom tooth removal a few years back. Took them for a day before switching to Ibuprofen. The damned room had started spinning when he was on the Vicodin.

"Doctor's orders. And no going to work for a few days."

"They need me."

"We need you healthy," Allie said.

"You sound like your mom. She would've said the same thing."

"She was smart."

"All right. I'll take a day off."

"Those things really killed all those officers?"

Rodgers nodded. He'd be hearing those screams in his head for a long time. "It was awful."

"What are you going to do about them? The things in the woods?"

"Going after them wasn't a great idea. I had a call with the chief. We're going to step up patrols for now. See if the state police will help and keep town safe."

"I don't suppose I can go anywhere?"

"You and your sister can take the bus to school on Monday. Come straight home."

"C'mon, the Bigfoot isn't going to chase down my car."

"I mean it," Rodgers said. "At least for a bit. Right home after school. Walk from the bus stop to the front door."

She did a patented Allie eye roll. Rodgers let it go. He was too tired and sore to argue. He had to keep the girls safe. Along with the girls, he had an entire town to look after.

For now, he closed his eyes and tried to forget the throbbing pain in his side.

Roland spent one of the more normal days he'd had in years with Alex. The weather people had forecasted more snow for tonight, making travel difficult. They'd decided to spend another night at the motel, just to be safe. During the day, they had lunch at a steakhouse. Roland had filled his belly with a porterhouse and a huge twice-baked potato. After that, they went to the outdoor store in town and got Roland some clothes.

Alex bought him jeans, heavy, socks, and a pair of boots. He also got some waffle-knit shirts, hat, gloves and a Carhartt zip-up hoodie.

He promised to pay Alex back once he started working. Alex told him not to worry.

They had dinner at a little mom-and-pop place called Lauren's. Fried chicken and mashed potatoes with peach pie for dessert. His belly near bursting, they returned to the hotel as the flakes started flying.

In the room, Alex turned on the television. The news was running a special report. Multiple state troopers had been killed by a Sasquatch. The pretty, brunette news caster actually used that word. Not an unknown assailant. Not an animal. Sasquatch.

The story cut to an anthropologist from the University of Buffalo who commented on the existence of the creature. It was being hailed as a major scientific discovery. Roland didn't care about that; he wanted to get away from Barker. The encounter with the creature still lingered in his mind. Leave the damned thing to the researchers.

"That's something, huh? Damn shame about those cops," Alex said.

"First UFOs and now Bigfoot."

"UFOs?"

"The government recently acknowledged their existence."

"Loch Ness Monster can't be far behind," Alex said. "I wonder if we'll hear anything outside, creeping around."

"Al, I should tell you something."

"Uh oh."

"I had an encounter with that thing the other night. In my tent."

"Seriously?"

"Dead. I had my tent set up behind the abandoned truck stop. I saw it. It was stomping around, trying to find me. I got the hell out of there."

"Why didn't you say something?" Alex said, sitting on the bed's edge.

"Now that it's out in the open, figured I'd tell you."

"Damn, that's scary. Did it chase you?"

"No, and I was able to hitch a ride to the Hope Center."

"Well we're getting out of here as soon as we can. No worries.

Roland hoped for an uneventful night. The hotel clerk's words echoed in his mind. Those things were around. What else would make the noises people heard? And now it sounded like the police had stirred things up.

One more quiet night, and then they'd be out of Barker.

Monique had spent most of the day resting after her ordeal. She'd gotten a text from Dr. Burrell a few hours ago. He would be a few days. Something had come up, and with the approaching bad weather, he didn't want to risk the drive. She would keep him updated on the research.

As she was watching TV – and the Sasquatch stories that had blown up on the news – Burrell texted her again. *Call me.*

James was watching a video on his iPad, earbuds in. She decided to take a walk, get out of the room for a bit. Monique waved to James, mouthed that she'd be right back.

Down the hallway, near the ice machine, she called Burrell.

"How are you doing?" he said. "I saw the news."

"Still a little shook up. Not sure what it wanted with me."

"The important thing is you're okay. Why didn't you tell me right away?"

"I was going to call you eventually. Didn't want to talk about it."

"This is an incredible event. You had direct contact with a Sasquatch."

"It wasn't all that, believe me."

"I'll be there as soon as I can. My mother got rushed to the hospital. Pneumonia."

"Sorry to hear that."

She was fine with him not coming up. Wasn't sure she still wanted to continue as a researcher. Trekking into the woods and thinking you heard vocalizations or wood knocking was one thing. Being grabbed and carried away was another thing. It had gotten too real. "I'm not sure I'll be here."

"What do you mean?"

"It's gotten a little intense. That was pretty bad, getting carried away."

"Did it hurt you?"

"No, but pretty sure it would've."

"And where did it take you?"

"Stuck me in this little hut made of sticks."

"Do me a favor. Write something up about this. Everything you can remember. Smells, sounds. Everything."

"I'm just gonna get some rest. Like I said, we might not stick around, James and me."

"Please reconsider. We're about to make history."

We. You're hundreds of miles away. I'm the one that almost died.

"I gotta go," Monique said. "Hope your mom is better soon."

She didn't give him a chance to answer and ended the call.

Back in the room, James was still watching his show. She waved at him, indicating he should take out the earbuds. He took them out and paused what he was watching.

"Talk to Burrell?"

"He's going to be delayed."

"That's a shame."

"I want to get out of here."

"The motel?"

"I want to go home. I'm done with this shit."

"You don't want to be a part of this? We have proof. *Real* proof."

"I almost died."

"I know, I know. You don't have to go back out there, though."

"For real?"

"Just saying you don't have to go out there. Plenty to do that's not field work."

He wasn't getting it. "I'm just done. This isn't exciting or fun anymore. I'm taking the truck in the morning. You and Kurt can come with or you can ride back with Burrell."

"Mon, take it easy."

"Watch yourself, James."

She wanted to get out of here, take a walk. Monique grabbed her coat and headed out. She wound up at the motel office. The clerk had her face in a smartphone. Monique stood in front of the counter for a moment before the clerk looked up.

"What can I do for you?"

"Is there a bar or restaurant within walking distance?"

"There's Brennan's. Turn right. Little ways down the road. You sure you want to go out in this?"

"I just need some fresh air."

"They have good wings. The Cajun barbecue are particularly good."

"Thanks."

Monique headed into the blustery night. She'd go, grab a drink and a bite to eat, then head back. The room had begun to feel like a prison, and James didn't seem to be listening. She walked along the shoulder, spotting the sign for Brennan's.

It wasn't far at all.

She crossed the parking lot. A few vehicles were parked out front. Neon beer signs filled the front windows. She'd grab a drink and head back to the motel. When she got back, James had better change his attitude. Either way, she was leaving in the morning.

She entered the bar. A few college-age kids gathered at one end, laughing and throwing back shots. She took a seat at the other end. The bartender came over. She wore a tight, black t-shirt with the bar's name scrawled on it and sprayed on jeans. Probably flirted for tips and made drunk guys think they had a chance with her.

"What can I get you?"

"Whatever house red you have."

"You got it."

A moment later, she came back with the glass of wine and set it on a napkin. Monique took a sip. It wasn't bad. She wasn't much of a drinker. Or a wine expert.

"Crazy about this Bigfoot stuff, huh? All over the news," the bartender said.

"Sure is."

"Staying in town?"

"Yeah over at the motel. I'm actually with a Bigfoot research team."

"No shit?"

"I shit you not. We've had a few encounters."

"You saw one? I love that kind of shit. Bigfoot movies, creepy stories on podcasts. Paranormal stuff, too."

"I was one of the people it grabbed and took in the woods."

"Seriously?"

Monique nodded and took a sip of wine.

"Your next drink is on the house. So what happened?"

Monique told her the story of being grabbed by the house and taken to the makeshift shelter in the woods.

"The cops are on edge. It killed some off them. Guess they're going to be watching for any of the things near town."

"Well I'm heading out in the morning. Not sticking around to see any more of them."

"It's a little scary. Exciting too, though."

"If that's what you want to call it."

"Let me know when you want that next drink."

The wine warmed her. She felt a little more relaxed. Maybe she would take that second glass on the house.

They'd let Gina see Steve for a few minutes. She'd held his hand. Tried not to break down. His head was bandaged and he hadn't woken up while she was at his bedside. The doctors were hopeful and the surgery had gone well. He'd have a long recovery ahead of him. After seeing Steve, she headed back to the hospital lobby, where Priya found her.

They hugged. Tears streamed down Gina's face. She couldn't hold them back. Priya's eyes were red-rimmed.

"How's David?"

"They're hoping he recovers. He might have some paralysis."

"Jesus, I'm sorry."

"How are you?"

Gina told her about being grabbed and hauled away by the creature. Then about her rescue. "What happened at the lodge after it grabbed me?"

"After it attacked Steve and David, I ran upstairs and hid. I heard it smashing around downstairs. It ran off after a while."

"They won't let us stay in ICU," Gina said. "I'm surprised they let me up to see him after hours."

"We can't sleep in the lobby. I grabbed my purse. I can get us a ride and try and find a hotel."

"That sounds good. I can pay you for the room."

"Your money's no good. I've got it."

They took a seat on the couches in the lobby. Priya set up a ride share for them, then booked a room at the motel just outside town. She was grateful to have a place to stay tonight. A warm bed. Though she wouldn't sleep well worrying about Steve.

Fifteen minutes later, their ride arrived, a silver Prius. They hopped in back. The driver was a thirty-something woman with blonde dreadlocks and a septum ring. The interior of the vehicle smelled like weed. She introduced herself as Fiona.

Jesus, I hope she's not high.

"You both in town long?" Fiona asked.

"Not long," Gina said. "Spending a few days."

"At the hospital?"

"We had an accident," Gina said. "Our husbands are hospitalized."

Fiona pulled away from the curb and they got on the road. The snow had picked up again. The oncoming headlights were dimmed by the storm.

"Hope we don't have any sightings, you know, Bigfoot?" Fiona said, giggling.

"You been smoking?" Gina asked. At this point, she didn't give a shit about being rude.

"Ha ha. Never on the job. Do you smoke?"

"Not since college," Gina said.

"Never tried," Priya added.

"You want to try, I can hook you up," Fiona said.

Her driving seemed fine. After a few minutes, they arrived at the motel, where Fiona let them out near the office. They went inside and checked in. Their room was at the far end of the motel, away from the office. The room had two queen beds. Priya took the one near the door. She was going to take a shower.

Gina kicked off her boots and lay on the bed. As the shower ran in the bathroom, she began to doze.

Jesse had been awoken by Rosco's whining. Normally, the dog slept like an entombed pharaoh, but tonight Rosco had been restless. Jesse's sleep had also been fitful. He'd rolled over, adjusted the pillow, thrown the covers off, put them back on. He decided to get up and read again. He looked at the clock. It was just past two in the morning.

He grabbed the journal and sat in the corner chair. Flipped to where he'd left off.

I'm home now. The final night at the site was something I never want to repeat. I'll likely never camp again. I retired to the tent around ten o-clock. I heard the first noises then. Sounded like someone was banging wood against a tree. A series of bangs, then it would be answered with more knocks and bangs. That went on for a while. The howls started after that. Same thing. Something howled. Then another animal answered.

It sounded too big to be a coyote. I was shivering at that point. Partly because I was chilly, but also scared to death. The howls started getting closer, and I wished I'd brought a gun. I was laying still, keeping my breathing even. Hyperventilating wasn't going to help my cause.

I'd hoped they would trail off into the distance, but things got louder. Closer. I killed the lantern I had shining in the tent. Didn't want to make myself any more visible.

The footsteps came closer. They were making a heck of a racket. At that point, I wiggled out of the sleeping bag. If I had to run, I didn't want to be stuck in the bag. I also grabbed my car keys and the small backpack I brought, which had this journal inside it.

I inched to the tent flap. They were all around the camp. I could smell them. Skunk smell seemed like perfume compared to the things outside the tent. I risked a look outside. I could see one of them outlined in the moonlight. It was huge and covered in dark, black fur. Makes a pro football player look like a dwarf.

Two more of them crashed around. I could hear them on the opposite side of the tent. I figured it was a matter of time before they realized I was in the tent. So I did the only thing I could do. I ran.

I broke from the tent. The large creature with the black fur turned and roared. I swear I felt the roar on the back of my neck. After I reached the woods, I zigged and zagged, keeping in the general direction of where I'd parked.

They came after me with a series of howls and screams. It was terrible. If they caught me, I knew I'd be ripped to pieces. I stopped twice and hid behind downed trees. At one point, I think they passed me. Eventually, I reached the truck. Threw myself behind the wheel and started it up.

One of them was coming. Saw it in the rearview mirror, a big, dark shape. I floored it getting out of there. Eventually it gave up and trailed into the woods. I didn't stop until I was home, and didn't care that I left my gear behind.

Jesse closed the journal. There were a few more sketches, a list of projects Dad had written down, with things like *Paint Fence* and *Replace Bathroom Faucet* scrawled in. After that, the remaining thirty pages were blank. Maybe the experience in the woods had soured him on journaling.

He dozed in the chair for a bit, woken sporadically by Rosco's whines. After he'd dozed for a while, Rosco barked as if a crew of burglars had broken in. He was at the bedroom window, paws up on the sill.

"What in God's name are you barking at?"

He got up and looked out the window. Damned snow was going crazy again. He couldn't wait for spring. Jesse squinted. Past the yard were the woods. The trees were rough shapes in the swirling snow.

Deep in the woods, something howled. One of those damned creatures. Jesse flinched. Rosco took his paws from the sill. Flattened his ears and started shaking. Jesse stroked his fur. "That's okay. We're safe in here."

He wasn't so sure about that. Not after the attack at his house.

Someone knocked on the door. "Come in."

Tim entered, wearing a red bathrobe. "Did you hear that, Dad?"

"I think the whole town heard it. Rosco's been going crazy."

"Is it them? The Sasquatch."

"It is."

Tim peered out the window. "I think I see something. Shit, it's coming out of the woods."

Jesse joined him at the window. In the snow, a big, dark shape emerged. Coming toward the house. "Is everything locked?"

"Yeah. I should wake Brian up."

"Go do that. Stay away from the windows if you can. Don't let it see you."

Rosco continued whimpering. He ducked into the corner between the chair and the wall. He couldn't blame the dog. Jesse didn't want to be here right now, either. Tim had never mentioned spotting a Sasquatch at the house. Why was one nearby now?

Tim came back with Brian, also in a robe. His eyes were half opened. "Is this for real?"

"It is," Jesse said. "What do you have for weapons?"

"Kitchen knives. The axe is in the basement with the camping stuff."

"Go get it," Jesse said. "Let's at least get some knives. Better than nothing."

"I'll call the police," Brian said, and took his phone from his robe pocket. He dialed emergency services and told the operator someone was outside the house.

While Brian was on the phone, Jesse went downstairs and grabbed a chef's knife from the butcher block. The lights were off in the kitchen, as well as the downstairs. Jesse remained still in the kitchen.

Brian's voice drifted from upstairs. He was still on the phone with the nine-one-one operator. Tim headed to the basement and returned a moment later with the axe.

"See anything?" Tim said.

"Nothing yet."

Brian padded into the kitchen. "They said they'll get here as soon as they can. They're getting calls all over town."

"That can't be good," Tim said.

"Sounds like there's more than one of them. Dammit. What's Rosco doing?"

"He's lying on the bedroom floor," Brian said.

"Rosco, come!" Jesse said.

He heard Rosco pad down the stairs. Jesse whistled and the dog padded into the kitchen, taking a seat at Jesse's side. Jesse scratched behind Rosco's ears.

"Brian, you should arm yourself," Jesse said.

"I don't know what a knife will do."

"Just grab something," Tim said.

Brian opened a drawer and took out a meat cleaver.

"Now that's a serious blade," Jesse said.

"Hopefully we won't need it."

The roar from outside told Jesse different. They exchanged glances. The Sasquatch was right outside the house. Jesse felt exposed in the kitchen. Two windows. That thing could bust through anywhere.

"You have glass block windows in the basement?" Jesse said.

"Why?" Tim said.

"Thinking we should head down there. Get out of sight."

"All right. Until the cops get here," Tim said.

The three of them – plus Rosco – headed to the basement. A neat stack of storage tubs stood in one corner. A Peloton Bike and some dumbbells took up another. The washer and dryer were in a separate room at the other end of the basement.

Rosco sat at Jesse's side, pressing himself into Jesse's leg.

"Maybe it was just passing by," Tim said.

Upstairs, glass broke. An angry roar followed the sound of breaking glass.

Laura Holtman glanced at the gas gauge every few seconds as she drove along Route 78. It was almost at E, and she had about ten miles to go before arriving home. After getting off her nursing shift at the hospital, she wanted to shower, get in her PJs, and slip under the covers. She cursed herself for not getting gas before leaving for work.

Luckily there was a 24-hour gas station and mini-mart up ahead. Although pumping gas in the freezing cold and blowing snow wasn't her idea of fun. She spotted the glow of the gas station lights. Eased the car into the lot, the car fishtailing in the slush.

The roads had a few inches of snow on them, and she hadn't seen a plow since leaving the hospital.

She hit the gas door button on the dash. She pulled up to the pump, got out, and flipped her fur-brimmed hood over her head. Screwed off the gas cap Inserted the card in the reader and after her card was approved, hit the 87 button on the pump. She stood with her back to the store, shuffling her feet and trying to generate some warmth.

The wind pushed against her back. When she was done pumping the gas, she put the nozzle back on the holder, facing the store. That's when she noticed the glass door was shattered.

Blood stained the white floor inside the store. A rack containing potato chips had also been knocked over.

She screwed the gas cap back on and shut the gas door. Had there been a robbery? What if the assailant were still around? The best course of action was to get to safety and call the cops.

She felt like someone was staring at her. Laura glanced at the front corner of the building. Someone huge stood there. Just watching.

"The hell with this."

As she moved for the car door, something screeched. It was damned big. There were reports of attacks on the news. She wasn't about to become a news story.

She threw herself into the car and hit the lock button.

As she started the car, she was aware of someone standing at the driver's window. She glanced and saw a massive, fur-covered torso.

This can't be happening.

A fist smashed through the window. The cold air rushed in. It grabbed her coat and yanked. Her head smacked the door. Dizziness danced in her skull. She gripped the wheel, hanging on.

The grip on her coat loosened, and then she was flung onto the ground as the creature ripped the door from the vehicle. Laura scrambled to her feet and stumbled forward in the snow. She heard the creature approaching, its feet crunching snow and ice.

As she tried to escape, it snatched her and lifted Lauren above its head. It seemed like she was impossibly high in the air. She kicked and flailed her arms. For a moment, she was suspended in the air, and then it slammed her to the ground. Something cracked in her back and a soundless scream escaped her throat. Pain off the charts.

The creature stood over her for a moment. Then it lifted its foot and the last thing she saw was the giant sole rushing toward her face.

Travis Kosowski's F150 sputtered. The dash lights flashed, and he steered it to the side of the road. He could see the lights in town. He was about a mile from the business district, marked by the Valero Station and Majestic Pizza. Damn thing had been acting up, and he had an appointment next week to have the truck serviced.

That didn't help him now. Especially in a snowstorm.

The proximity of the town seemed to be mocking him. It was damned close. He could walk, hit an all-night diner. Fill up on hot coffee and pastry. He was returning from working on a construction job in Watertown. He'd headed out late at night, tired of the hotel that smelled like feet and wanting to curl up next to Samantha. His girlfriend would be worried.

He took out his cell and dialed her number.

"Hey babe," she said in a sleepy voice. "Where you at?"

"Truck broke down. A mile out of Barker."

"I told you to get it looked at sooner."

"I had this little thing called a job to go to."

"Still, you always put things off. Did you call Triple-A?"

"Right after I'm off the phone."

"You safe?"

"I'm good. I can wait in the truck. Almost made it."

"Hurry home."

"I'll do my best. I'll keep you posted."

He called Triple-A and it was a two-hour wait. Damn winter. That was plenty of time to walk to Macey's Diner and back. It was one of the only twenty-four hour joints he knew of. Just a few cups of coffee, maybe a slice of blueberry pie. He didn't care if it had been sitting there all day.

He could deal with the snow during a short walk. Travis got out of the truck and started down the road. The whipping snow felt like tiny pebbles on his face. He lowered his head and pushed forward.

When he was about halfway to town, he became aware of someone behind him. Heard footsteps. Travis turned and didn't see anything. He went farther and heard the footsteps again. This time, he also heard a low growl.

He'd never considered the possibility of a wild animal, although the road was flanked by heavy woods. "Back off, whatever you are!"

The animal growled. The sound sent a chill through Travis. He broke into a jog.

Not that far to town. If he could get to the Valero station, he could duck inside the store there. Whatever was behind him picked up the pace. He glanced over his shoulder.

It was on two legs, and impossibly big. Covered in reddish-brown fur. Maybe someone was playing a horrible prank and had him on video.

The creature caught up and grabbed his jacket. It tossed him and he landed in the middle of the road, his weight on his arm. Something popped in his forearm and he screamed. The beast approached, and

Travis scooched away, aware that he could be run over by an approaching vehicle.

The thing stomped on his lower leg, and the bones snapped. He looked down at his ruined leg. The bones had poked through the skin and his pants. He began to weep from the pain.

The monster lifted him by the front of his jacket. He was face-to-face with it, smelled its rotten breath. It scowled at him, a look of almost human hatred on its face. Then it opened its mouth, cocked its head, and bit into this throat. Something crunched, and then breathing became impossible.

Twenty

Rodgers' phone rang, jolting him out of his sleep on the couch. He answered. It was the Chief.

"Just filling you in. We had another call. Noises outside a home out on Branch, off Seventy-Eight."

"I can come in," Rodgers said.

"Nonsense. You have broken ribs."

"It's not that bad."

"Rest up and then get back with us. I'll keep you updated."

"I feel useless."

"Quit feeling sorry for yourself. Or I'll stop over and kick your ass. The girls okay?"

"They're here with me, yeah."

"Best stay put. And keep your Glock handy. We're getting reports all over town."

How many of those things were there? A whole family of the bastards, apparently. "Will do."

Rodgers got off the phone and willed himself to his feet, pain spearing through his torso. The girls were still asleep. From the bedroom, he grabbed his Glock and a few extra magazines. He sat on the couch, which faced the front windows.

The snow looked pretty. Prettier because he didn't have to be out in it. He didn't do any winter sports and didn't understand why people went nuts for skiing and snowboarding.

Right now, it was quiet here. As he watched the falling snow, he decided to keep the girls home for a few days. At least until this settled down. Safer that way.

He felt useless. Like tits on a bull, as his grandmother was fond of saying. Hopefully things would stay quiet. He stared at the falling snow and tried to ignore the pain in his ribs.

One glass of wine had turned into three for Monique. The bar was warm and felt almost cozy – of course that could've been the wine. Outside, the storm howled. It wasn't the best idea to walk up here, but she could always text James to come and pick her up. The bar was getting close to having last call. She'd have to leave soon.

Her phone dinged. She looked at it. A text from James.

Where you at?

The bar right down from the hotel.

Hearing noises. People are freaking out.

Come pick me up.

K. Be a few. Have to clean off truck.

The noises. They close?

Pretty. Whole motel is awake.

Monique paid her tab, excluding the free wine the bartender had given her. She slipped her coat on and headed for the front door, where she watched out for James. Ten minutes later, he pulled up with Kurt in the passenger's seat.

The only other people left in the bar were the bartender and an elderly man in a trucker's cap. Monique waved to the bartender, who said, "Stay warm."

In the backseat, she said, "When did the noises start?"

"Right before I texted you. Howls. Growling in the woods."

"Dammit. If the weather wasn't bad I'd say we should just take off."

"You're right," James said.

"About time you admitted it. Change your mind?"

"I don't want to be around if those things come calling, but we're stuck," James said. "You shouldn't have gone off like that, Mon."

"I'll go where I please. Next time, maybe listen to me."

Kurt said, "Can we save the lovers' quarrel for another time?"

"Watch yourself," Monique said.

"I don't mean to interfere, but the guns are at the motel. We might need them," Kurt said.

James got them through the snow. Back in the motel room, Monique heard people buzzing in the hall. She poked her head out the door and saw a handful of guests milling around. A few were still in pajamas and robes. Kurt had gone to ready the guns. James was peering out the window when Monique entered the hall.

Monique approached a fifty-something woman in a plaid robe and bear slippers. "What's going on?"

"The most horrible howls are coming from outside."

"How close are they?"

"Too darn close."

"I'd recommend you lock yourself in your rooms."

"You some sort of expert?"

"I have first-hand experience with a Sasquatch."

"A Sasquatch? Like the abominable snowman?"

The woman must be from out of town. Didn't know the town's reputation. "Like that."

"What would they want with a motel? Are they aggressive?"

"Can be."

Monique left the woman and the other guests. She went to the motel office, which was dark. No sign of the clerk at the desk. "Anyone here?"

The clerk poked her head up from behind the counter. The glow from the computer monitor illuminated her face. "Those howls are fucking terrifying."

"Did you call anyone?"

"Called the Barker P.D. They're swamped with calls. No one's coming right away."

"Our group has guns. If it comes to it, we'll drive them off."

"This is wild," the clerk said.

"What's your name? I'm Monique."

"Alicia."

"Is the door locked?"

"On it," Alicia said. She rounded the counter and locked the door. It was all glass. Not much good, but they had to take every precaution they could.

While they stood in the lobby, a long, drawn-out yowl came from outside. It sounded like they were getting close. Monique said to Alicia, "You should come away from that door."

Roland had woken up about forty-five minutes ago. Several of the creatures had opened up with howls and screams. Alex had jumped out of his bed, stubbed his toe, and done a little dance, exclaiming, "Fuck, fuck fuck." His toe swelled up and had started to turn purple. He was currently sitting in one of the chairs, foot up on a stool.

Another howl, this one long, came from outside.

"Jesus, that's unnerving," Alex said.

"Try seeing one of them. It's even worse."

"What do they want?"

"Don't know. Let's hope they don't come close."

The room had two doors: one that led to the parking lot, and another leading into the hallway. Roland heard people in the hallway. He went to investigate, leaving Alex and his busted toe in the room.

A half-dozen people had gathered in the hallway. A grizzled guy in jeans and a sheepskin collar jean jacket was among them. He had a large revolver in a leather holster on his belt. Roland thought the man looked like he could've taken on the James Gang back in the Old West.

A young, black couple stepped from their rooms. The woman had a semiautomatic pistol in a holster. The young man had a short-barreled shotgun. Why would they have guns with them?

Roland approached the woman with the pistol. "What's with the guns?"

"We're Bigfoot researchers. We come prepared."

I've got a story to tell you. Some other time. "Hope it won't come down to using those."

"Agreed. Monique. This is James, and that geezer there is Kurt."

"Roland. I'm here with my brother Alex. He's back in the room."

Nearby James and Monique stood a woman with a septum piercing and dyed blue hair.

"Anyone know if this place has a room with no windows? Or some type of basement?" Roland said.

The woman with the blue hair said, "There's a laundry. We also keep the maid's supplies there. But we won't all fit. There's room for maybe five or six people."

"Worth asking."

Monique said, "Everyone should get in their rooms and lock up."

A young, shirtless guy said, "What good's that going to do?"

"People standing in the hallways and panicking isn't helping," Monique said. "Everyone should go back. We'll keep watch. We have the guns."

"Ya'll should listen to her. She knows what she's talking about," James said.

The shirtless guy frowned, crossed his arms. He was maybe in his twenties. Had a full six-pack and looked like a gym rat. A woman his age came up behind him. She had on a tank top and high-cut shorts. She also looked very fit.

"This is bullshit. You should give me one of those guns," shirtless said.

"You ever fired one?" Monique said.

"How hard can it be? I'll pop a cap in whatever's out there."

"C'mon Dylan," the woman said, tugging his arm. "I'm cold."

Roland said, "Everyone should head back. If Monique and her friends need to use those guns, we should be out of the way."

"Whatever," Dylan said, and drifted down the hallway with his girlfriend.

Roland figured the guy was trying to look hard.

"Did anyone call the police?" an elderly woman in a puffy robe said.

"I did," the blue-haired woman said. "They aren't coming anytime soon. Lots of calls in town."

Something smashed glass down the hallway. It sounded like it was coming from the lobby. The breaking of glass was followed by more screams, although this time the horrible noise pinged off the walls. One of them had broken in.

The remaining guests in the hallway scurried like rats on the run from an exterminator. The woman in the puffy robe fell and slapped against the rug. An elderly man with a liver-spotted scalp helped her up, and they hustled back to their room. Within moments, the hallway was empty, save for Roland and the gun- toting researchers.

"You should probably clear out, Roland," Monique said. "Thanks for your help."

Something else broke in the lobby. Sounded like furniture smashing. Roland retreated to the room, where he found Alex still in the chair.

"What's going on?"

"Three armed guests in the hallway. And one of those things just broke in."

"Jesus. We should try and run for it."

"In this weather? Plus, they're outside the motel. We wouldn't get fifty feet."

"So what do you suggest?"

"Hunker in and hope they defend us out there," Roland said, nodding in the direction of the hallway.

"Not a great plan."

"What else do we have?"

Rodgers awoke to the sound of something being turned over outside. He sat up too fast and was rewarded with pain blasting through his side. "Dammit."

He grabbed the Glock, sat and listened. He didn't hear anything for a few moments, and then the hallway light flipped on. Allie appeared in the living room.

"Dad, I think someone's outside," she said.

"Did you hear what I just did?"

"There was a shadow across my window."

Rodgers got off the couch, feeling like he needed a crane to move him. "Wake your sister up and come right back."

"Ok Dad."

Allie must be scared. He rarely got an "Ok Dad" as an answer without some sarcastic remark. Rodgers went to the front window. Beyond was the snow-covered lawn and the vehicles in the driveway. Nothing else out front.

"Was this necessary?" Hannah said, entering the living room. Allie followed her.

"I want us together. Have a seat on the couch."

Both girls plopped on the couch, Hannah sighing.

"Anything out there?" Allie asked.

"Nothing out front. Going to check the back bedrooms."

He proceeded to the rear of the ranch, first ducking into the room that had served as Skylar's office. He didn't come in here often. Occasionally, he seemed to get a whiff of her perfume. It brought memories of her crashing back.

The room's only window faced the back yard. He peered out. The storage shed seemed undisturbed. Other than the shed, the yard was a quilt of snow. He went into the girls' room, again, somewhere he rarely ventured. Nothing on that side of the house. The side yard leading the Goldman's house was clear.

Lastly, he slipped into his bedroom, noting he had a basket of laundry to fold and put away. The curtains were drawn across the window. He drew the curtains. In the driveway stood a massive Sasquatch. It turned its shaggy head and stared at him, baring its teeth.

Startled, Rodgers stumbled and fell back on the bed. He winced at the pain in his side. The Bigfoot smashed its fist through the window. On his back, facing the window, he fired twice.

The beast yelled in pain as the rounds punctured its chest. It retreated from the window, then smashed its fist against the house. At least he'd hurt it. He managed to get on his feet. Snow blew through the window.

Allie ran in the room. "Are you okay?"

"I'm fine. Get back in the living room. It's right outside. I shot it twice."

Rodgers hobbled around to the door, and together he and Allie returned to the living room. He couldn't defend the house for long if multiple creatures showed up. Plus, he still had to worry about the one he'd shot.

He took out his phone and handed it to Allie. "Call Nine-One-One. I know they're getting calls all over, but at least they know we're in trouble."

Allie dialed.

Rodgers wasn't worried about the broken window. It was too small for a Bigfoot to enter. There were still plenty of other ways to get in.

While Allie was on the phone, Rodgers checked the front window again. He saw the Sasquatch round the corner. It was coming toward the front door.

"Girls, it's coming. Get behind me."

Rodgers aimed at the front door. The Sasquatch slammed into the door twice and it blew open. The beast ducked inside. Blood matted the fur on its chest. The Sasquatch roared. One of the girls clenched

Rodgers' shirt. He shot the Sasquatch twice in the face. It backed through the door.

Rodgers advanced. Its jaw hung in tatters. He aimed for the temple and fired multiple rounds. Bone splintered and brain spattered into the creature's fur. It staggered and fell forward in the snow.

He turned and saw the girls standing right behind him. "Get my keys for the SUV off the hook, Allie. We're getting out of here."

"Can you drive?"

"No, but you can."

Twenty-One

Allie grabbed the keys and all three of them put on winter gear. Rodgers heard more howls and roars in the distance. The creatures weren't close to the house. They might have time to get away. He was going to head right to the station. They would be safe there.

Rodgers closed the front door. The Sasquatch had busted the lock, but he could at least shut it. He and the girls stood on the front steps. The Sasquatch lie face-down in the snow, its arms spread out, as if being crucified.

"Ugh, that thing reeks," Hannah said.

"Not as bad as your breath," Allie said.

"Stop it. Not the time or place," Rodgers said.

A few inches of snow covered his patrol SUV. He wasn't about to clean it off, given that creatures could be lurking. The windshield wipers would have to suffice.

"All right, follow me."

He stepped off the porch. Pain flared in his side, and he doubled over.

"Dad, let us help you," Allie said, and looped his arm around her neck.

"You're a good kid."

Hannah got on the other side, and he leaned on his girls until they reached the SUV. It made him feel better knowing the shotgun was in the vehicle, as well. Allie and Hannah helped him into the passenger's seat. Hannah sat in back, behind the partition that separated the front and back seats. She bitched a little about feeling like a criminal. Rodgers rolled his eyes at that.

Allie got behind the wheel and started it up.

"Just take it easy. She's got four-wheel drive, but that won't stop you from skidding in the snow."

"Got it," Allie said.

She backed out of the driveway and got them on the road.

Jesse waited for a while with Tim and Brian in the basement. The howling continued outside, but nothing had entered the house. Jesse began to think they'd dodged the creature, but then a huge bang came from upstairs. He'd been sitting on one of the storage totes and jumped up at the noise.

Rosco began to whine again. Jesse scratched behind his ears.

Heavy footsteps slapped the floor above.

"It's in the house," Tim whispered.

Rosco growled this time, finding some courage. Jesse petted him and said, "Shhhh. Good boy."

The footsteps were overhead, in the kitchen. It occurred to Jesse that the basement door had no lock. Not that it would've stopped the monster for long. Just the idea of a lock provided some small comfort.

It stopped right outside the door. Jesse could hear the creature's heavy breathing. If it opened that door, all they had was an axe and knives. Might as well attack it with toothpicks.

The doorknob turned. That sent ice through him. How did it know to open a doorknob?

The door eased open. A fur-covered arm reached inside, felt around.

"Get under the stairs," Jesse said.

The three of them and Rosco ducked around the staircase and got under it. There was enough room for them to crouch. Thankfully, Tim and Brian hadn't stored anything in this area.

Jesse got a whiff of the beast. Damned pungent. It took a step, covering multiple stairs at once. The steps had no risers on them, so they could see its massive leg and foot.

The step cracked, then split in two. The beast's leg slipped between the stairs, and it roared in surprise. Jesse stabbed its leg. Another howl.

Brian followed suit, hacking the creature's calf repeatedly with cleaver. Blood flowed and dripped on the concrete.

Rosco snarled, finding his bravery. The snarls turned into aggressive barking. The Sasquatch lost its balance, one foot stuck under the stairs, and fell sideways on the steps, so that its leg was wedged. It splayed out on the stairs at an odd angle.

Jesse and Brian continued hacking at its leg. Tim gave a yell, popped out from under the stairs, and swung at it with the axe, burying it in the creature's arm. Another roar, this time of pain.

Tim pulled the axe back. As he raised it to strike another blow, the Bigfoot swatted him, and he smacked the floor, dropping the axe. Jesse rushed to Tim and scooped up the axe. He got a look at the creature. Its chest was bleeding. Bullet wounds. Someone had taken a few shots at it.

He dropped the knife and landed a blow, this time, severing two of the monster's fingers, which plopped on the basement floor. Under the stairs, Brian continued chopping, face dotted with the creature's blood.

Maybe it was weak enough from the bullet wounds that they could finish the monster off.

The Sasquatch jerked, wood splintering, and it freed itself, rolling off the stairs with a thud. The creature's blood slicked the basement floor. It had to duck under the joists to avoid hitting its head.

Jesse stood before it, holding the axe. Tim got back on his feet. Brian ducked out from beneath the stairs. For a moment, the creature glared at Jesse. There was fury in its eyes. He was likely about to have limbs torn off.

It stood between him and the stairs. Brian flanked the Sasquatch on the left, and Tim on the right. There'd be no getting around it.

A steady drip-drip of blood came from its severed fingers.

Jesse raised the axe, ready to fight, even if it meant dying. The creature swatted him, clipping the side of Jesse's head. He crashed into the wall. Rosco snarled.

He looked up and saw Brian rush in with the cleaver. The Sasquatch flung him against the wall. Brian's skull cracked against the concrete. He slumped to the floor. Tim screamed and backed toward the stairs. Brian lay unconscious. Blood streamed from his mouth. His jawbone had dislocated and twisted.

Jesse gripped the axe. His stomach swirled. Head pounding, he got up. The creature had its back to Jesse. Mustering what he had left, Jesse screamed "Run!" as he slammed the axe between the monster's shoulder blades.

Tim made eye contact with Jesse.

"Go! Take Rosco!"

The creature attempted reaching behind it to remove the axe embedded in its back. It still stood between Jesse and the stairs. Tim called Rosco, and the dog skirted the creature, following Tim up the stairs.

Rosco paused at the top of the stairs, barking, seeming to urge Jesse to follow. He would be in good hands. Tim had inherited Jesse's love of dogs. Rosco was the fifth dog Jesse had owned in his lifetime, and the third since Tim was born.

Tim grabbed Rosco's collar and urged him along. If he didn't get out of here, at least Tim and Rosco would be safe.

The Sasquatch whirled around, the axe still jutting from its back. Jesse backed away from it, until he butted against stacked boxes. In his younger days, he might've tried slipping past it, but his days as a high school point guard were long gone.

The Sasquatch approached, a growl forming deep in its chest. He closed his eyes as it landed a blow to his skull, and the world went dark.

Gina was glad she'd grabbed the guns before leaving the lodge. The animal sounds had started outside the motel a while ago, and she'd heard glass shattering and yelling. She stood at the door, listening.

Priya stood behind her. In the distance, sirens wailed. A firetruck's horn blatted. Sounded like total chaos out there.

"Hear anything?" Priya asked.

An ear-shattering roar drifted down the hallway. Their room was at the far end of the motel, farthest from the office.

"That sounds like it's inside."

Gunshots rang out in the hallway. An angry howl followed the shots. There was a door heading out the lot, but they had no vehicle. She wasn't going to take her chances on foot against a Sasquatch. She'd seen what they could do.

Shouting came from the hallway. More gunshots. Getting closer.

Monique, James, and Kurt opened fire on the Sasquatch that barreled down the hallway. It was huge, like the others, with reddish-brown fur. They'd scored a hit, but the creature hadn't slowed. They couldn't stay in one spot, so they retreated to their room, Kurt joining them. He was the last one in, and locked the door.

"To the lot. We get in the truck and go," Monique said.

"What about the other guests?" James said.

"We can't save everyone," Kurt said.

"Hopefully the cops get here."

Monique flung the door to the lot open. Behind her, the room door was ripped open. She heard it smash against the wall. Kurt and James slipped out behind her. Never thought to ask if James still had the keys. He did, and he hit the button on the fob. The locks clicked open.

Behind her, the Sasquatch thumped on the door. It would be out here in seconds. James got in. The creature ripped open the door and ducked through, just ten feet from the truck. She blasted it, the Sasquatch staggering forward, bleeding.

Kurt fired the shotgun. The gunshots were murdering her hearing. Ears ringing, she watched the creature's face explode, bits of bone and flesh scattering. The shotgun blast had blinded it, and it staggered, swiping blindly at things. She almost felt sorry for it. Kurt racked the gun and shot it again.

James hopped out of the car, and together they joined in, emptying their magazines into the creature. It fell in the snow, the bright, red blood mixing with the fresh powder.

Monique breathed a sigh of relief. They'd stopped the creature. She still wouldn't feel safe here. A few guests opened doors and peeked out. A man with bright red hair said, "That's the damndest thing I've ever seen. Look at the size of him."

Monique holstered her gun. They were going to pack up and go home tonight, snow or not. Or at least stay in another town. At the far end of the motel, two women stepped outside, one of them carrying a semiautomatic pistol. Must be a theme at this motel, bringing guns.

The women approached. The one with the gun was petite and dark haired. Her friend was darker-complected, her long, black hair pulled back.

"That the only one?" the woman with the gun said.

"Don't know, but I'm not hanging around to find out," Monique said.

Down the hallway, it had sounded to Gina like the motel was being ripped apart. She and Priya had waited in the room after hearing the roars and gunfire in the hallway. The source of the noise shifted, and then gunshots came from outside. When they'd stopped, Gina risked a peek outside, easing the door open. She spotted the monster lying dead in the snow, and a trio of armed guests nearby the fallen beast.

She and Priya had decided to approach. Now, the creature was sprawled in the snow, its brownish hair matted with blood. It smelled worse dead than alive, if that were possible.

"That the only one?" Gina said.

"Don't know, but I'm not hanging around to find out," the woman said.

"James, Kurt, we're out," she said.

"Mon, you sure you want to get on the road?" James said.

"You sure you want to wait if more of them show up?" Monique said. "Pack up. Like I said, I'll take the truck if you're staying."

"I'll get my gear," the older guy with them said.

The trio headed inside, leaving Gina and Priya standing in the lot near the dead Sasquatch. She was impressed they'd brought it down. Sirens wailed in the distance, drawing closer to the motel. A moment later, a police SUV rolled into the lot and stopped twenty feet from the dead creature.

Gina realized she was holding the semiautomatic. She set it on the ground and backed away.

The officer got out, drew his gun. "Step back, both of you. Hands where I can see them."

The officer approached the dead Sasquatch. A moment later, another patrol vehicle pulled in, and a second officer hopped out.

The first cop said, "Wait over by the building. Did you shoot it?"

"The people in room One Seventeen. They were out here with guns."

"Jesus, it's a shooting gallery," the first cop said. "Guess it's good someone had guns."

Gina hoped this was the end of the creatures.

The howls coming from the surrounding woods told her differently.

Roland allowed himself hope when he heard the sirens. He went to the window and saw the flashing cruiser lights. Two police vehicles were parked in the lot, and two women stood nearby. A dead Sasquatch lay in the red-tinged snow.

His mood deflated when he heard more howls. He turned to Alex, who was lying on his bed. "Maybe we should risk a drive."

Alex sat up. "What's going on out there?"

"Cops. Someone bagged one of the monsters."

"More howls outside. I think your right, brother. Let's get our shit together and go."

Alex got up, hobbling from the broken toe. He grabbed his jacket and slipped into his boots. Roland grabbed his things. "I'll call the motel when we're on the road and settle up for the room. They have my card on file."

"Don't think they're worried about it right now," Roland said.

They hopped into Alex's vehicle. He started it up, letting the heater warm up, while they brushed snow off. It was still dark, and the snow made visibility poor, but Roland was glad to be leaving.

The police were hunched over the body of the dead monster, examining it. The two women were heading back inside. Alex steered them out of the lot and hit the road. He kept it at around twenty miles an hour, and they pulled out of town, ending up on the long stretch of Route Seventy-Eight that offered little more than a view of the pines.

"We'll just keep her steady. Might take us a bit, but we'll get home. I'll make us a big-ass breakfast."

"Alex. Stop. Look."

"What?"

Alex had been looking at Roland, chatting. He looked straight ahead and saw what Roland did. A large Sasquatch standing in the middle of the road. Fur black as diesel exhaust. It watched the vehicle as if daring them to advance.

"Shit."

"What are you going to do?"

"Maybe it's just crossing the road."

"It's not moving."

"I'll turn around," Alex said.

"Do it quick."

Alex began his turn, crossing the double-yellow line and getting them headed toward town. Roland looked out the back window. The creature broke into a run. "It's coming. Speed the hell up."

"Trying. It's goddamned slippery."

Alex hammered the gas. The wheels spun in the slush. They were going twenty. The tires began to grab, and they lurched ahead. The Sasquatch was gaining, maybe fifty feet away, and the SUV skidded to the right, the back end wobbling. The delay allowed the Sasquatch to reach them. The SUV jolted to a halt.

It had grabbed the rear bumper. Roland lunged forward as the creature bellowed and lifted the vehicle's rear off the ground. Alex hit the gas. The tires whirred and spun in the snow.

The SUV tilted to the right. Roland was thrown against the door, and then they were upside down and skidding. The SUV slid, smacking into a tree. He glanced at Alex, who had cut his head. Blood dripped onto the vehicle's interior roof. Roland was held in place by the seat belt, as was Alex.

The creature approached. It ripped Alex's door off and flung it. Alex screamed and scrambled to unclasp his seatbelt, although Roland was unsure why. The creature, hunkering down, grabbed Alex, who reached for Roland.

Roland grabbed his arm, digging into his jacket. The creature jerked Alex through the door, snapping his leg in the process. Alex's screams filled the air. Roland pushed against his door. It would be impossible. Upside down and pressed against a tree, he was helpless.

The most horrible, high-pitched screams came from Alex, punctuated by the creature's roars. They stopped, and he saw Alex's lifeless body hit the ground in front of the vehicle.

He would be next.

Roland pressed his hands against the roof. How long could he remain upside down in the vehicle? Would someone find him? First, he had to hope the Sasquatch wouldn't kill him. It had just slaughtered his brother in a matter of minutes.

He heard it stomping around, circling the vehicle. It bashed the outside of the SUV and growled. Getting frustrated. The creature's face appeared in the driver's side window. It had bent down and was staring at him. The Sasquatch reached inside, but couldn't get to him.

Its hand was inches from him. He pressed himself against the door, trying to maintain distance. The creature wiggled its arm, stretched and tried to grab him. After a few moments, it gave up and withdrew its arm.

The Sasquatch pounded on the vehicle a few more times, and then he heard it stalk off. He waited for a few minutes, expecting an attack. It had gone.

Now he had to figure out how to escape the vehicle.

The sun rose, and the snow began to clear. Sunbeams pierced the vehicle's windshield. Roland didn't know how long he'd been inside the SUV when he heard a vehicle come to a stop.

"In here! I'm in here!" he said, and pounded on the door.

A young woman appeared in the driver's side window. She was on her hands and knees. A soft "Omigod" escaped her lips.

"Are you hurt?" she said. "I was on my way to work when I saw your car. What happened to that other man?"

"One of the monsters got him. It might be in the area."

"I'm calling for help now. Hang tight," she said, and stood up. He heard her on the phone. A moment later, she ducked down again, phone still to her ear. "Help's coming. They want to know if you're injured?"

"Banged my head, but nothing other than that."

"They're on the way."

A moment later, he heard sirens. They grew to a crescendo, and from his vantage point, he saw a heavy rescue fire truck pull up, along with a police car and an ambulance. Firefighters in turnout gear hopped out of the truck and approached the car.

A police officer stood over Alex's body. The young woman approached the officer and was saying something, pointing to the vehicle.

Roland closed his eyes. He was saved. Couldn't say the same for Alex. He felt responsible. After all, Alex had come here to pick him up. If he'd stayed put, Alex would've been alive. He should never have come. Roland could've stayed at the Hope Center for a while.

"Hey buddy, we're gonna get you out of there, okay?"

Roland glanced at the driver's side window, where people kept appearing like it was a drive-thru window at McDonald's. The firefighter in the window gave him a thumbs-up.

"Hurry if you can."

"You got it pal."

It took a bit to extricate him from the vehicle. The whine of saws cutting filled the air. He thought maybe they used the jaws of life at one point. When they put Roland in the ambulance, he noticed they'd thrown a sheet over Alex's body. His brother had been reduced to a bloody lump in the road. Poor Alex, who'd drank his first beer with Roland. Had snuck him into *Porky's* when they were fifteen. The first time he'd seen a naked woman anywhere, on film or in person.

Alex, who'd been a star baseball player in high school, throwing smoke and striking out batter after batter. He'd been scouted. There'd been talk of him playing college ball, but never came to fruition. His brother was always bringing home stray dogs and volunteering at food drives. A much better human than Roland, who'd faded into the streets. Now Alex was gone. Died horribly.

Roland didn't want to think about the sounds he'd made as he died.

The ambulance sped to the hospital. They unloaded him and wheeled him into the emergency department. At least the blankets they'd given him were nice and warm. A pretty triage nurse took his vitals and asked him a bunch of questions. Then they moved him into a bay in the emergency department.

A doctor came in and examined him. They ordered a CT for his head, which still throbbed from knocking it on the roof. He got his CT Scan a while later, then sat in the bay. They decided to keep him overnight, and sometime early that morning, he got sent up to a room. Once they got him settled, another doctor came in, an Asian man with salt-and-pepper hair. Informed Roland he had a slight concussion, but nothing serious. Did a quick neuro exam on him and left Roland.

The nurses came in to check and take vitals for what seemed like every few minutes. He just wanted to sleep. Then he had to think about his next move. He told one of the nurses he was homeless and had no family. Only brother had been killed.

The hospital had a social worker on staff. They'd be sending her in to talk to him.

He was getting off the streets. Away from Barker. Didn't know how yet, but he'd do it. For tonight, he'd rest his head. Solutions would come when he felt better.

The police had asked Monique and the others questions about the creature attacking the motel. They checked to make sure the three of them had their pistol permits. After that, they were free to go. They got the truck packed up in record time and were on the road, listening to the occasional howl echoing through the woods.

The town of Barker had a problem. Who knew how many of the creatures were still out there? As they were driving out of town, two news vans passed them. This would dominate the news cycle, the discovery of Sasquatches and real-life battles with the monsters. Until America got bored and the next event took its place in the headlines.

She texted Ballard and told her she was finished being part of the team. James could do what he wanted. If he wanted to risk his ass out in the woods, so be it. Ballard had called twice, and she let it go to voicemail. That would be him trying to convince Monique to stay on the team. He had the video clips, and she'd write up reports for him before leaving.

James was behind the wheel. "You good?"

"I'm done with this."

From the back seat, Kurt snored.

"For real?"

"For real. Not dying in the name of research."

"This is huge. You don't want any part of it?"

"Not worth it. You want to keep going, do it without me."

"Not the same without you. If you're out, I'm out."

He reached across the console and took her hand.

"Sometimes you're not so bad," Monique said.

"Not so bad," he said, chuckling. "Suppose I'll take that."

"Keep your eyes on the road. Get us home in one piece."

Gina and Priya managed to get a ride share to pick them up from the Bigfoot motel – at least that's how she thought of it. They got a room at a place in the next town, ten miles down the road. They'd work on getting a rental car so they could get back and forth to the hospital. There was still the insurance mess with both their cars.

As they'd left the motel, more police vehicles had pulled in. State police and county sheriff's vehicles. A helicopter whirred overhead, and the media had set up with their trucks on the road. The police had set up barriers to keep them back.

She'd called the hospital to check on Steve. He was stable and resting comfortably. Gina didn't know what this would mean for the restaurant. She might need to take some time off and leave Antonia to run things. Steve's recovery was the most important thing now.

The motel they'd picked was quiet and clean. No screams or howls from outside. No need to keep a gun at the ready. There was a café across the street from the motel. Her stomach growled.

Priya lay on her bed, eyes closed.

"You want to get a bite?"

"I'm starving."

"We should call our friends. In the chaos I never thought to call them and tell them about their home."

"I'll need to get our Jeep out of there somehow," Priya said.

"Yeah, I have to find out about our Kia, too."

"Let's worry about that later. Get a bite and get to the hospital?"

"That sounds good. New day."

One in which she wouldn't have to run for her life.

Rodgers sat propped in a chair in the squad room. The girls had helped him inside once they'd reached the station. They were currently with Ginny Helgas, one of the rookies, getting some hot chocolate. Phones buzzed in the squad room. Cops went scrambling. The chief himself was headed out to the motel outside town. The things had attacked, and a motel guest had allegedly bagged one of the beasts. Calls had come in all over town. Sightings. Attacks. It was general chaos.

He felt useless, like a starter sitting out the Super Bowl. This was huge. A nationwide story documenting the existence of Sasquatch. It was going to be crazy dealing with the media.

Plus, they still had the creatures to contend with. The State Department of Environmental Conservation was en route to Barker. The Feds were headed here, and it was rumored National Geographic was sending a film crew. The Governor was on his way from Albany, and they'd be getting some help from the National Guard.

The pain in his ribs was all-consuming. He couldn't get comfortable. Despite shifting in different positions, the pain flared, a steady pulse of agony. In the rush to escape the house, he hadn't grabbed pain meds.

Ginny returned from the break room with the girls, both carrying steaming mugs of hot chocolate.

"How you doing, Lieutenant?" Ginny said.

"Feel like someone's stabbing me with a hot poker."

"That good, huh? Sorry we don't have something more comfortable."

"It's not a hotel," Rodgers said. "I'll survive."

"What's going to happen now?" Allie said.

"We wait it out here until it's safe to go home," Rodgers said.

Hannah said, "When will that be?"

"When we're not going to get attacked in our own house. The Guard's on the way. Tons of police around. They'll get the town secured."

Ginny said, "What are we going to do about Them?"

Rodgers shrugged. "No idea. Give out hunting licenses? Preserve them as a species?"

This was uncharted territory. He imagined there'd be battles between people wanting to hunt the creatures and those wanting to study them. Let them fight it out. For now, he was glad the girls were safe. That's what mattered.

He closed his eyes and tried blocking out the pain in his side.

Anthony Izzo is the author of over 30 horror and dark fiction titles. He enjoys writing tales of mayhem involving anything from zombies to psycho killers to murderous shapeshifters. Anthony has also served as a judge for the Buffalo Dreams Film Festival screenplay competition. Anthony holds a B.A. in English from D'Youville College in Buffalo, NY. When not writing, he likes playing loud guitar, drawing, and spending time with family. He makes his home in the Western New York Area. Visit his website for updates and newsletter signup at www.anthonyizzo.com.

Did you love *Ravaged*? Then you should read *The Foundation*[1] by Anthony Izzo!

[2]

Dylan O'Connor's life is about to be turned upside down. Saddled with medical debt from his daughter's cancer treatments, he receives a letter from a mysterious Foundation offering financial assistance. All he has to do is complete some seemingly routine tasks and the Foundation will help with his bills. Dylan soon finds out the required tasks are dangerous and illegal. The Foundation begins playing a twisted game with him. A game that could cost him and his family their lives.

The only way out for Dylan is to play the game to its gruesome end.

A thrilling novel of dark suspense from the author of Nightshade and The Lacerated Sky.

Read more at www.anthonyizzo.com.

---

1. https://books2read.com/u/38Qgna
2. https://books2read.com/u/38Qgna

www.ingramcontent.com/pod-product-compliance
Lightning Source LLC
LaVergne TN
LVHW021607310326
835206LV00038B/1185